FHIR KYA HUA

CASE I

GAURAV SINGH NEGI

Made with ♥ on the Notion Press Platform
www.notionpress.com

"TO MY FAMILY AND FRIENDS"

Contents

Acknowledgements

I would like to express my sincere gratitude to everyone who supported me during the journey of writing this novel.

First and foremost, I am deeply grateful to my parents, my father Mr. Kripal Singh and my mother Mrs. Shanti Devi, for their unconditional support, encouragement, and belief in me. Their patience and trust gave me the strength to follow my passion for writing.

I would like to thank my brother, Devendra Singh, for his constant guidance, creative ideas, and valuable help in editing. His insights and honest feedback played an important role in shaping this story.

I would also like to thank all my friends who continuously motivated me and believed in my work, especially Bhavya, Mohit, and Arnav, along with many others whose support meant a lot to me. Your encouragement helped me stay focused and confident throughout this journey.

Lastly, I thank every reader who chooses to read this book. Your time and interest give meaning to this story.

This novel marks the beginning of my journey as a writer, and I hope it connects with you.

— Gaurav Singh Negi

CHAPTER ONE

Inspector Veer Singh

I was sleeping in my room when suddenly the light turned on. "Who is this?" I said, feeling a bit annoyed because I was in a deep sleep.

"It's your housemaid, Priya, sir," a soft voice came from the door.

"It's time to wake up, sir," she said.

I checked my watch. It was 9:00 AM already. Oh no, I slept more than usual. I quickly got Up, went to the bathroom, brushed my teeth, took a fast shower, and changed my clothes. I Combed my hair, put on my shoes, and grabbed my bag. Priya had kept tea and breakfast ready on the table. I drank the tea quickly and ate some bread with butter. Then I picked up my car keys and went out. As I drove the car out of the gate, the guard saluted me nicely.

(Now you are thinking why this guard is saluting me, right?)

So,

Hi, my name is Veer Singh, and I am 27 years old now. I am an IPS officer. I love to solve cases. In my job, I have solved many cases like murders, missing people, scams, thefts, and many more. Every time I solve a case, it feels good because I help people get Justice. I did my schooling in Uttrakhand. There, the school was in the hills, and I used to walk a long way every day. The air was fresh, and we spent a lot of time outside. Then I went to college in Delhi. Delhi was very different—big roads, lots of traffic, many people everywhere. I studied hard there and prepared for my IPS exam. Now my posting is in Mumbai. Mumbai is very big and famous, but it has a lot of crime. Every day, many cases come to the police station. Theft, fights, cheating, all kinds of things happen here. I don't know why people commit crimes to earn money. Doing bad things to others for money is not right. If you work honestly, you can live a good life.

I remember when I was a child, there was a police officer named Manoj in our town. Everyone respected him a lot. He helped poor people, stopped fights, and kept the area safe. I always wanted to become like him. When I cleared my IPS interview and got selected, my whole family cried with happiness. My father looked at me with so much pride in his eyes. That day was the best day of my life. Anyway, now I will tell you about my family. There are 4 people in my family.

First, my mom, Ritu Devi. She is very extroverted. She can talk to anyone easily. One day, She went on a flight alone, and when she came back, she had made 10 new friends. She talks to strangers like she has known them for years. Whenever she sees a single girl anywhere, she starts thinking about my marriage. She gives them my full details—my job, my age, everything. When she calls me, first she asks about my health, but then mostly she talks about girls only. She sends me photos of girls every week, saying, "See this one, she is good." She loves cooking. She tries new dishes every day. But my favourite is her aloo-paratha. When I was in school, my friends always asked me to bring aloo-paratha in my tiffin because it was so tasty. Mom is good at everything—cleaning house, taking care of us, making everyone happy.

Second, my dad, Rakesh Singh. He is very innocent and hardworking. When I was small andgoing to school, he used to have a 9-to-5 job in a private company in Uttrakhand. He worked very hard to give us good food, clothes, and education. Now I have a good job, so I tell him many times, "Papa, leave your job and come live with me in Mumbai." But he says no. He loves our old house in Uttrakhand. He says all his childhood memories are there—the games he played, the trees he climbed, the festivals with neighbours. He doesn't want to leave it. In his free time, he tells us stories from his old days. We all sit together and listen. It feels nice. Dad also likes traveling. In summer holidays or winter breaks, we used to go to different places. Sometimes hills, sometimes temples, sometimes beaches. We made many happy memories on those trips.

Third, my brother, Mohit. He is younger than me. I don't like him sometimes because he argues with me about every small thing. If I say something, he says the opposite. He is not good at studies. He always gets only passing marks, even if we tell him to study more. In school, he used to fight with other boys every day. Teachers complained a lot. But he is very good at sports. He plays cricket very well. He got selected for the city cricket team many times. He hits the ball far and bowls fast. Maybe one day he will play big matches. Even if we fight, he is my brother, and I care for him.

Oh, we have reached the police station now.

I parked the car and went inside. The constables saw me and saluted. I went to my office and sat in my chair. There were some files on the table. I started signing papers and checking reports from last night. After some time, Sub-Inspector Dev came into my room. He was talking about a theft case.

"Sir, he is very clever. Every time we make a plan to catch him, he runs away before we reach him." Dev said.

"Dev, now criminals are smart. They think fast and stay one step ahead. You have to try something new to catch him. By the way, what is his name?"

"Raj Sharma, sir."

When I heard the name Raj Sharma, my heart started beating very fast. My face changed a little. Old memories came back to my mind.

"What happened, sir?" Dev asked.

"Nothing," I said. I took my pills from the drawer and ate one. After 2 minutes, my heart became normal again.

"Is everything good, sir?"

"Yes, I just... leave it. You go now."

"Okay, sir, I am leaving," he said and went out.

I sat there thinking for some time, but then I started work again. After some hours, a big luxury car stopped in front of the station. One man, a boy, and one woman came out. The woman was crying a lot.

"Ma'am, what happened? Please stop crying and tell us," Dev was saying outside.

I came out and asked, "What happened?"

"Sir, they are very upset. They are not telling properly."

"Send them to my office," I said.

"Okay, sir."

They came into my office and sat on the chairs. The woman was still crying.

"First, drink water. Calm down and then tell me what happened," I said. I gave them water glasses.

The boy stood up and said, "Sir..., my name is Anil, and I am 18 years old. Something is not good. My best friend.....and their son have been missing since yesterday." He said intentionally

"What? Tell me from the start," I said, taking interest

CHAPTER TWO

FLASHBACK

Anil speaks:

We are four friends—Ajay, Sonam, Sital, and me. We have all been best friends since 2nd grade. We studied in the same school from the beginning, sat on the same benches, played together during breaks, and shared everything. Now we are all in 12th grade, and these days feel like the best time of our lives. We laugh a lot, tease each other, help with studies, and always have each other's backs. No matter what happens, we know we can count on one another. But everything changed on December 18th, around 11:30 PM...

I was sitting in my room, trying to prepare for my pre-board exams. I really hate chemistry. Why are there so many things to remember? There are reactions, equations, periodic tables, everything mixed up in my head. And only 10 days were left for the exams. On top of that, I couldn't focus at all because of our school volleyball tournament. I was the team captain, so the pressure was high. I wanted to win badly for the school team. I was talking to myself while turning the pages of my chemistry book. "Come on, Anil, you have to remember this... why is this so hard?" I muttered, rubbing my eyes because they were getting tired.

Then my mom entered my room with a glass of milk.

"Sleep early, beta," she said softly. "Tomorrow is your big match, and I don't want you to lose because you're tired."

"Yes, Mom, I am just finishing this page and going to bed. Good night," I replied with a smile.

"Good night, beta," she said, kissed my forehead, and left the room, closing the door gently.

I closed my books, kept them on the study table, and jumped onto my bed. I felt a little relaxed now. I took out my phone and started scrolling through reels—funny videos, dance clips, everything to relax my mind before sleeping. That's when, suddenly, a message popped up on our group chat from Sital.

Help me! Call me, please, it's an emergency.

My heart skipped a beat when I read it. Sital never sends messages like this. She is usually the calm one in our group. I immediately called her number, but the call didn't connect, it just kept ringing. I tried again, same thing. No answer. I quickly started a group call. Ajay and Sonam accepted almost right away.

"Guys, did you see what Sital messaged in the group?" I said as soon as they joined.

"Yes! What happened? Did you call her?" Sonam asked, sounding worried.

"I tried twice, but the call is not connecting. Does anyone have her house's landline number? Maybe her mobile is off or something," I said.

"I think I have it saved. Let me check and try," Ajay said.

We waited for two minutes while he dialed.

"No one is picking up the landline either," Ajay said, his voice a bit tense.

"Oh! How did I forget this?" Sonam said suddenly, sounding calmer now.

"What? What happened?" I asked quickly.

"Relax, guys. The day before yesterday, Sital told me in secret that she wanted to prank you both. I think this is just her prank," Sonam explained.

"What? A prank? Are you sure?" Ajay asked, surprised.

"Yes, I'm pretty sure. That's why she's not picking up the phone or landline. She's probably hiding and laughing right now," Sonam said confidently.

"But what if it's not a prank? What if she really needs our help?" I said. I was still feeling uneasy. Sital is our friend, something could be wrong. Just then, another message from Sital came in the group, a dead skull emoji.

"What the... a dead emoji now?" Ajay said, reading it out.

"See? Look what I said, it's definitely a prank. If she was really in trouble, why would she send silly emojis instead of calling the police or explaining properly?" Sonam said.

I thought about it for a second. Sonam had a point. Sital loves doing small pranks sometimes.

"I think you are right," I finally said, feeling a little relieved.

"Okay, guys, let's just see tomorrow at school. We'll ask her directly," Ajay said.

"Yes, and Ajay, don't forget, tomorrow is our big volleyball match too," I reminded him.

"Buddy, I know! I'm excited. See you in class tomorrow," Ajay replied.

"Good night, everyone," Sonam said.

"Good night," we all said, and the call ended.

I put my phone on charge, switched off the light, and tried to sleep. But honestly, that message stayed in my mind for some time. I kept thinking if it was really a prank or not. But Sonam's words made sense, so I pushed the worry away and finally fell asleep.

The next day,

I woke up 30 minutes earlier than usual. I wanted to be fresh for the volleyball match, so I did some light yoga in my room—stretching, breathing exercises, everything to feel energetic. After that, I went for a short morning walk around our society. The fresh air felt good, and I listened to some motivational songs on my phone. When I came back, I took a nice bath, wore my school uniform, packed my sports kit, and had breakfast—toast, eggs, and juice that Mom had made it.

My father had gifted me a car when I turned 18 last month. It's a simple white sedan, but I love driving it. I usually take it to school now instead of the school bus. It makes me feel grown up. I drove to school that day, parked in the student area, and walked toward the class.

As I entered the classroom, I saw Sonam and Ajay already there, standing near the window and talking seriously about something.

"Hey, guys! What's up? What are you both discussing so early?" I asked, dropping my bag on my bench.

"Nothing much, Anil. We are just making plans for today's party," Sonam said with a big smile.

"Which party? You didn't tell me anything," I said, surprised.

"My mom and dad are going out for some office work, they have a late-night meeting and won't be back till morning. So, we thought, why not have a small party at my house tonight?" Ajay explained excitedly.

"Okay, then count me in! Sounds fun," I said. We all high-fived.

"Buddy, are you excited for today's volleyball match?" Ajay asked, punching my shoulder lightly.

"Yes, super excited, but I'm also a bit nervous. I'm the captain, you know, so everyone is looking at me to lead," I admitted.

"Chill, bro. We have practiced so much. We will win for sure," Ajay said confidently. He's also on the team, so he knows the pressure.

"By the way, where is Sital? She's usually here by now," Sonam said, looking around the class.

"I don't know. Maybe stuck in traffic," I replied. Just then, the classroom door opened.

"Hey, guys!" Sital said cheerfully as she entered, looking completely normal with a big smile on her face. She kept her bag and came toward us.

"What are you guys planning?" she asked curiously.

"First, you tell us—why did you send those scary messages in the group last night? And why weren't you picking up our calls?" I asked directly.

"Sorry, guys. I didn't pick up the phone because for the last 3 days, I haven't been able to sleep well. Too much study stress, I think. So yesterday, I took some sleeping pills that my Mom gave me and went to bed really early," Sital explained calmly.

"Oh, okay. But then how did you send those messages?" Ajay asked, looking confused.

"What are you guys saying? Which messages? I don't know anything about any messages," Sital said, looking genuinely surprised.

"Oh, come on, Sital. What do you think—we are kids anymore? Stop the acting," I said, a little annoyed now.

"No, guys, I swear! I really don't know what you're talking about. I slept early and woke up fresh. Today," Sital insisted.

"Sital, now stop it. The prank is over. Anyway, are you coming to Ajay's house tonight for the party? His parents are out, so we're planning food, music, everything," Sonam said, changing the topic.

"I will try to come," Sital replied with a small smile.

Just then, the bell rang for the first period. Everyone rushed to their seats. Sital went to her bench quietly and sat down, looking like she was thinking about something deeply. She kept staring at her notebook without writing anything. Ajay and I had to leave for the volleyball match—it was during school hours, so we grabbed our kits and headed to the ground with the team. The match excitement was building up, but somewhere in my mind, Sital's words were still confusing me.

CHAPTER THREE

The Night

School finally ended, and we had lost another volleyball match. It hurt a lot. I am the captain of the team, so it was hitting me the most. Everyone was looking at me, and I felt like I had let the whole team down. If we lose just one more match, we will be disqualified from the entire tournament. All our hard work, all the early morning practices, everything would go to waste. I couldn't stop thinking about it.

I was driving back home in my car, feeling really low. The roads were busy as usual, but my mind was somewhere else. I kept replaying the match in my head, what I could have done better, where we made mistakes. My serves were off, the blocks weren't strong enough, and the other team was just too good today. I sighed deeply, gripping the steering wheel tightly.

When I reached home, I parked the car and went inside.

"I am home, Mom," I said, trying to sound normal.

"How was your match today, beta?" Mom asked from the kitchen, coming out with a smile.

"We lost another one," I replied, putting my head down on the dining table. I didn't want her to see my disappointed face.

"Oh, don't take so much pressure. It's just a game," Mom said softly, putting her hand on my shoulder.

"But Mom, I am the captain. If we lose the whole tournament, everyone will blame me. The team, the coach, even my friends—they all expect me to lead properly," I said, feeling the weight on my chest.

"Okay, captain, now change your mood a little. Tell me, do you want to eat something? I made your favourite pasta today," she said, trying to cheer me up.

"No, Mom, I'm not hungry right now. Or wait—by the way, we friends decided to have a party at Ajay's house tonight. So please don't call me there, okay? We'll be busy."

"Okay, beta, but you have to come back before 12:00. If not, I will call you then," she said strictly but with love.

"Okay, Mom, before 12:00, I promise," I replied, giving her a small hug.

I went upstairs to my room, closed the door, and lay on the bed for a minute. Then I took out my phone and opened our group chat.

"Hey guys, are you excited for today's party?" I wrote, trying to forget about the match.

"Of course! By the way, which movie do we watch tonight?" Sonam replied quickly.

"Horror!" Ajay replied with a dead skull emoji.

"Okay, but first you go and practice more for the next volleyball match," I wrote back, still a bit upset about the loss.

"Anil, I told you before—I was trying very hard in the match. What do you think, we are losing because of me?" Ajay replied, sounding angry.

"I am not saying we are losing because of you. I am the captain, and I just want everyone to give 100% in the next match. We can't afford another loss," I explained.

"Okay, guys, stop fighting now. Keep the tournament aside and get ready for the party. It's going to be fun!" Sonam replied, always the one to calm things down.

I kept my phone on the side table and opened my books to study. Exams were close, and I needed to focus. I studied chemistry for some time, trying to remember those reactions again—but my mind kept going back to the match and the party.

After a few hours, I checked my watch. It was 7:30 PM already. Time to get ready. I went to the bathroom, took a nice warm bath to relax my body—it felt good after the tiring day. Then I changed into casual clothes—a cool t-shirt and jeans. I put on some deodorant and combed my hair. Feeling fresh now.

I picked up my phone again and wrote in the group: "All ready?"

"Yes, already! My parents have gone to their office work. When are you guys coming here?" Ajay replied.

"Just leaving my house," I wrote back.

"And what about you, Sonam and Sital?" Ajay asked.

"Same here, just leaving," Sonam replied.

"I am also leaving in 10 minutes," Sital wrote.

"I am leaving, Mom!" I shouted while going downstairs.

"Okay, beta, have fun. And remember your promise, before 12:00, okay?" Mom reminded me from the living room.

"Yes, Mom, I know. Don't worry."

I wore my favourite shoes. The black ones that look cool and took my bike out from the garage. I usually take the car to school, but for short trips like this, the bike is faster in traffic.

After about 20 minutes of riding, I reached Ajay's house. The streets were lit with lights, and some people were walking around. I parked my bike outside his gate and started walking toward the door. That's when I saw Sonam already standing outside the house, looking confused.

"Hey, Sonam! What are you doing standing outside?" I asked, coming closer.

"See for yourself," she said, pointing at the main door.

I looked properly, there was a big lock on the door. The house looked completely closed.

"Where did he go? He said his parents are out and we're having the party here," I said, surprised.

"Don't know. Maybe he went to buy something," Sonam replied.

I took out my phone and called Ajay, but his phone was switched off. It went straight to voicemail.

"His phone is switched off," I told Sonam.

"Now what do we do?" she asked, looking worried.

"I think he is out to bring snacks or cold drinks for the party. Let's wait a bit."

"Yeah, I think so. Let's wait," she agreed.

We stood there talking about school and the match for some time. After a few minutes, Sital also reached by taxi.

"What happened, guys? Why are you both outside?" Sital asked, Taxi leaves.

I explained everything—the locked door, Ajay's phone off.

"Oh, strange. Maybe he's coming soon," Sital said.

We waited together, chatting to pass the time. But after 30 minutes, I started getting angry.

"What is this! Where is he? It's almost an hour now," I said, feeling frustrated.

"This is not fair. He called us here for the party, and now he's not even here. Where did he go?" Sonam said, also annoyed.

"I am waiting for the last 10 minutes only. Otherwise, let's go somewhere else. I am feeling very hungry now," I said, rubbing my stomach.

"Yes, you are right. Last 10 minutes—it's too late already," Sital agreed.

We waited another 15 minutes, but still no sign of Ajay. No message, nothing.

"Okay, now it's over. I am not waiting for him anymore. I am going," I said finally.

"Yes, I am also coming with you," Sonam said.

"You guys go. I am not coming—I am going back home," Sital said quietly.

"At least come and eat something with us," Sonam tried to convince her.

"No, guys, I am not feeling good today. My head is aching a little," Sital replied.

"Okay, if you are not feeling good, you can go home and rest. Take care," I said.

Sital ordered a cab and left. Sonam and I decided to go eat something.

"Now, where do you want to go?" I asked Sonam.

"I am feeling very hungry. Let's eat something nice," she said.

"Yes, me too. Let's go to Ruby Café—it's nearby, and their food is good."

"Okay, let's go!" We went to Ruby Café on my bike. It was a small, cozy place with nice lights and music. We ordered pizza, hot coffee, momos, and French fries. The food came hot and tasty. We ate slowly, talking about funny school memories and forgetting about Ajay for some time. It felt good to eat after waiting so long.

After eating everything, I dropped Sonam off at her home safely. Then I rode back to my house. I checked my watch—it was 10:30 PM. I went inside quietly.

"Oh wow, Anil! You are back before 12:00. It's the first time you kept your promise properly." Mom said, surprised and happy, from the sofa.

"But you came so early—what happened? Party over already?"

"Mom, I am feeling so sleepy. I will tell you everything tomorrow, okay? I am going to bed now," I said, yawning.

"Okay, beta, good night. Sleep well," she replied.

The next morning, my phone rang early. I was still half asleep. I checked—it was Ajay's father calling.

"Hello, Uncle, good morning. Do you need any help?" I said, sitting up in bed.

"Beta, is Ajay at your home? He didn't come back last night," Uncle said, sounding worried. My eyes opened wide in shock. "What! He hasn't come yet?"

"What are you saying? What happened?" Uncle asked, his voice rising.

"Wait, Uncle, calm down. I am going there right now. I will tell you everything."

I quickly got ready, brushed my teeth, and drove fast to Ajay's house. When I reached, Uncle and Aunty were standing outside their home, looking very tense.

"What happened? Where is Ajay? Tell me what you were saying on the phone," Uncle asked as soon as he saw me.

I told them everything that happened yesterday—the party plan, the locked door, waiting for an hour, his phone off, and how we finally left.

Aunty started crying. "Where is my son? He never does like this!"

"Let's go to the police station right now," Uncle said, wiping his eyes.

"Yes, Uncle, you are right. We have to file a complaint immediately," I agreed, my heart beating fast.

CHAPTER FOUR

24 HOURS

Present day:

"That's all, sir. Now, please find my friend as soon as possible," Anil said, his voice shaking a little. He looked really worried, like he had lost his brother.

"Oh, so you are saying that your friend called you guys for a party and then just went somewhere else without telling anyone?" I asked, making sure I understood everything correctly.

"Yes, sir," Anil replied, nodding quickly.

"But sorry, Anil, we can't file a complaint before 24 hours of missing time are complete. That's the rule for adults," I explained calmly.

"What do we do now?" Ajay's father asked, looking helpless and frustrated.

"Nothing much right now. We have to wait for 24 hours. What if he comes back home on his own? Many times, young boys go out with friends and come late," I said, trying to give them some hope.

"But sir, he never goes out without telling us for so long," Ajay's mother said, starting to cry softly. Tears were rolling down her face.

"Ma'am, please don't cry. Think positive. He might be safe and just forgot to inform," I said gently, offering her a glass of water.

"I think, sir, is right. What if he comes home before 24 hours?" Anil said, trying to support his friend's parents.

"I just pray to God that he comes back home safe before that," Ajay's mom said, wiping her tears. Then Anil and Ajay's parents stood up slowly. They thanked me and left the station quietly, looking sad and tense. As soon as they went out, Dev turned to me.

"Sir, why are these rich people so panicked like this?" Dev asked with a small smile.

"Their son is missing from last night, Dev. Anyone would panic," I replied seriously.

"But they have to wait 24 hours anyway," he said.

"I already told them the rules."

"What if their son doesn't come home even after 24 hours?" Dev asked.

"Yes, I am also thinking the same. This case is interesting—a boy plans a party, calls his friends, and then suddenly vanishes. No trace, phone off, house locked. We have to keep an eye on it," I said.

Just then, my phone started ringing. I checked the screen—it was my mom calling.

"Okay, sir, now I am leaving," Dev said. He saluted me properly and walked out of my office.

I picked up the call. "Yes, Mom, how are you?

"Good, beta. How are you? Are you working on any big case, or just sitting in your room doing nothing?" she asked in her usual teasing way.

"Mom, I am an IPS officer. The whole of Mumbai's crime responsibility is on my shoulders. What do you think—I am just sitting idle?" I replied, smiling to myself.

"I know, beta, I am just kidding with you," she said, laughing softly.

"So, what are you doing right now?" I asked.

"Nothing much. Trying to make a new dish in the kitchen. Today I am experimenting with Some paneer recipe," she replied.

"Oh, you and your new dishes. One day you will make something that even I can't eat," I joked. Then she said excitedly, "I have good news for you!"

"No, Mom, I don't want to talk about girls right now," I said quickly, knowing her habits.

"What?" she said and started laughing loudly. "No, beta, I am not talking about girls this time!"

"So, what is the good news then?" I asked, feeling curious.

"Me and your father have decided to come visit you in Mumbai!" she said happily.

"Wow, that's great news, Mom! When are you coming?"

"We are thinking that Mohit's winter break is also starting shortly, so we will come after that. All three of us—me, Papa, and Mohit."

"Great! I am also missing your handmade aloo-parathas so much. Here in Mumbai, nothing tastes like home food," I said, feeling happy thinking about it.

"Anyway, what about that photo I sent you yesterday?" she asked suddenly.

"Which one?"

"Don't be over smart, beta. I sent you a girl's photo yesterday for marriage!"

"Oh, that one. Yes, I saw it."

"So, will you text her to meet or not?"

"Mom, every girl looks beautiful in photos with filters. First, I will meet her, then decide," I said honestly.

"Okay, beta, first meet her, then decide. But don't delay too much."

"Okay, Mom, I have to go now. Some work is pending."

"Okay, beta, bye. Take care and eat properly," she said, and the call ended.

I put the phone down and started doing my other work—checking files, signing reports, and talking to other officers about on going cases.

At night, I checked my watch. It was 9:00 PM already. Time to go home. (What happened to Ajay? Did he come back home or not?) I kept thinking about the boy's case while walking out.

I picked up my car keys and drove to the market first. I needed vegetables and some other things for dinner. The market was still open, with lights and people buying stuff. I bought fresh tomatoes, cucumbers, carrots, yoghurt, fruits like bananas and apples, and some milk.

Today, I decided to make a fresh salad with curd and a fruit shake for dinner. (By the way, when I was a kid, I used to help my mom a lot in the kitchen—cutting vegetables, stirring things, even making rotis sometimes. So now I know how to cook most things by myself. Living alone in Mumbai, it helps a lot.)

I reached home, parked the car, and went inside. First, I took a relaxing bath to wash away the day's tiredness. The warm water felt good. Then I changed into comfortable home clothes and went to the kitchen.

I started preparing dinner—chopped the vegetables neatly for the salad, mixed them with salt, lemon, and some chaat masala. Then I made a simple curd raita and blended the fruits with milk for a thick shake. It looked healthy and tasty. I put everything on the dining table nicely. I switched on the TV and started watching the breaking news channel while eating. There were reports about traffic, some political news, and a few crime updates from the city. Nothing major today. The salad was fresh and crunchy, and the shake was cool and sweet. Eating alone is quiet, but sometimes it's peaceful.

After finishing dinner and cleaning the plates, I remembered that Mom had sent me a girl photo. I took out my phone and opened the chat with the number she gave.

"Hey, I am Veer. My mom told me about you." I sent the message.

After a few minutes, she replied: "Yes, my mom also told me about you."

"You are also living in Mumbai, right?" She asked.

"How did you know?"

"My father told me," She replied.

"Oh, okay. So where are you living right now?"

"Mulund," she wrote.

"And you?"

"Chembur. It's only 18 km from Mulund. So, can we meet sometime?"

"Yes, why not? I know the best place called 'The Food Studio'. The food and ambience are nice there."

"Okay, sounds good. Today is Friday, so I think Sunday is perfect."

"Sure, Sunday is done. Let's meet in the evening?"

"Okay, bye for now."

I kept the phone on the side table, took my medicine pills— the ones for my heart rate—and went to bed. I thought about the day, the missing boy case, and now this meeting on Sunday. Life as a police officer is never boring.

Next morning,

I woke up at my regular time, around 7:30 AM. The sun was coming through the window, and I felt fresh.

Priya, my housemaid, came to the room with tea.

"Sir, I want a leave today," she said politely.

"Why? What happened?" I asked, sitting up.

"Sir, my sister's health is not good. The doctor said she has to rest completely, and there should be someone to take care of her at home."

"Oh, okay. You can go. Family comes first," I said.

"But, sir, what about cleaning the house and cooking?"

"No worries, Priya. I will manage everything myself. You go and take care of your sister."

"Thank you so much, sir," she said gratefully, with a big smile.

"Okay, now I have to get ready and go to the station."

I drank the tea, got ready quickly—bath, uniform, everything—and took my car to the station. At the station, I sat in my office and signed some more documents. There were reports from night patrols, some small theft cases, and routine paperwork. Time passed slowly. Then, after some hours, I heard a car stop outside. I looked through the window—it was the same luxury BMW from yesterday. Anil and Ajay's parents entered the station again, looking even more sad and tired this time.

"Sir, 24 hours have been completed now, and Ajay still hasn't come home," Anil said directly, coming to my desk.

"Did you call everyone—his other friends, classmates, relatives?" I asked.

"Yes, sir, I called everyone I know. No one has seen him or heard anything," Anil replied.

"Sir, please, I request you—find my son. He is everything for us," Ajay's mom said, her eyes full of tears again.

"Yes, ma'am, don't worry. We will do our best to find him," I assured her.

"Dev!" I called. Dev came running.

"Take their full statements properly and file the missing complaint now," I instructed.

"Yes, sir," Dev said and took them to another table to write everything down.

(After a long time, another proper missing person case. I think this time I will solve the full case and give everyone justice. I won't repeat the same mistake from the past again.) I thought to myself while watching Dev write the file.

CHAPTER FIVE

The Investigation Begins

[24 hours after the missing report]

"First, give me all the details of Ajay—like his phone number, recent photos, and if he has any vehicle, then photos of that too," I said, opening a new file on my desk.

"Okay, sir," Ajay's father replied quickly. He took out his phone and started sharing the details with Dev, who noted everything down.

"Now, tell me everything about Ajay. His nature, hobbies, favorite places—anything that can help us understand him better," I said, looking at Anil and the parents.

"Ajay is a very extroverted and obstinate boy," Anil started. "He always does what he wants, no matter if it's good or bad. Once he decides something, it's hard to change his mind."

"Yes, he is right," his parents added together. His mom nodded, looking proud but worried at the same time.

"Any bad habits? Like smoking or drinking?" I asked carefully.

"No, sir, never!" his mom said quickly, sounding shocked. "He is just a student. Why would he do these things?"

"Sorry, ma'am, but in investigations, we have to know everything. Even small details can help," I explained politely.

"Any girlfriend?" I asked next.

Anil looked at me and gave a small sign with his eyes, glancing toward Ajay's parents. I understood immediately—he didn't want to say it in front of them. I requested Ajay's parents to step out of the room for a minute.

"Uncle, Aunty, can you please wait outside for just a bit? I need to ask Anil some private questions. Questions about school friends," I said.

They agreed without any argument and left the room, closing the door softly.

"Yes, sir, he has a girlfriend. She studies in our school only, but in a different section," Anil said quietly once we were alone.

"What's her name?"

"Tamanna," Anil replied.

"Does she know that Ajay is missing?"

"No, not yet. But it's been more than a day now—she will find out soon when he doesn't come to school or reply to messages."

"Do you know anything else about Ajay that could help us? Any secrets or problems?"

"Yes, sir. He gets upset very easily."

"Like he has anger issues?"

"Yes, sometimes. If things don't go his way, he can get really angry fast."

"Oh, thanks for telling me this, Anil. It might be important."

I called out, "Dev, send Ajay's parents back inside."

Ajay's father came in first. "Sir, did you find anything new?"

"No, not yet, sir. But I want to ask you something. Is there any issue in your family? Like, do you think any relative could be involved in this?"

"No, sir, never," his father said firmly. "All our relatives love Ajay a lot. He is like a favourite in the family. No one can do anything bad to him."

"Thanks for clarifying. Now you can leave. If we find anything, we will inform you immediately. And always stay alert—if there is any call or message from a kidnapper or anyone suspicious, tell us first, okay?"

"Yes, sir," his father said.

"Sir, please find our son," his mom said again, with tears in her eyes as they stood up to leave. I called some constables and instructed them to go with Ajay's parents to their house.

"Check the house properly, look for any clues, and take more information about Ajay's daily routine."

"Not you, Anil. We need your help here to find him," I said when Anil started to leave with them.

"Okay, sir," he replied, looking serious.

Ajay's parents left the station with the constables.

"Sir, my mom doesn't know about all this yet. So can I tell her that I am helping the police to find Ajay?" Anil asked.

"Yes, go ahead. Do it fast—then we have to start searching," I said.

He nodded and moved to a corner to call his mom. I checked the time—it was 12:00 noon already. The day was moving fast.

"Dev, I need Ajay's phone records as soon as possible," I instructed.

"Yes, sir," Dev said and started making calls to the mobile company.

"Let's go, sir," Anil said, coming back after his call.

We sat in the police jeep with two more constables. Anil guided the driver first to the houses of Ajay's nearest friends. We visited three or four homes, talked to their parents and siblings, but no one had seen or heard from Ajay since that night. Everyone looked surprised and worried.

After that, Anil suggested we check Ajay's favorite places—the spots where he liked to hang out most of the time. First, the library near their school, where he sometimes went to study or read comics. The librarian said he hadn't come in the last few days.

Then we went to a couple of cafés—small places where they ate snacks after school. The owners knew the group of friends, but said Ajay wasn't there yesterday or today.

Next, the sports ground where Ajay sometimes played cricket. A few boys were practicing, but none had seen him. We checked a gaming parlor and even a mall nearby, but still nothing. No one knew where Ajay was. Anil was getting more tense with every place.

When we were moving to the next location, my phone rang suddenly.

"Sir, we found something important," one of the constables from Ajay's house said excitedly.

"What is it?" I asked.

"Sir, Ajay's house has CCTV cameras installed outside and in the compound. We can check the footage from that night!"

"Good work! I am coming there right now," I said.

"Okay, sir."

"Driver, turn around—move to Ajay's house fast," I ordered.

"What happened, sir?" Anil asked, looking hopeful.

"We found CCTV at his house. We can see the footage from the day he went missing," I explained.

"Oh yes! How could I forget about those cameras? They installed them last year after a small Theft in society," Anil said.

After about 15 minutes, we reached Ajay's house. One constable was standing outside waiting for us.

"Yes, where is the CCTV footage?" I asked.

"Come with me, sir," he said.

We entered the house. Ajay's parents were sitting in the living room, looking tired and sad. The constable opened a laptop connected to the security system and started playing the footage from the previous evening.

I watched carefully. First, I saw Ajay coming out of the house around 7:30 PM. He was wearing a white t-shirt with a brown jacket and black pants. He looked normal, waved at the camera maybe, took his bike from the garage, and left.

After some time—about 20-30 minutes later—a girl came and stood outside the gate. She was waiting, checking her phone. Then Anil arrived on his bike and joined her. In the end, after another 20 minutes, one more girl came and joined them. The three waited together, talking sometimes, looking at the door. They stayed till around 10:00 PM, then finally left one by one.

"Who are these girls?" I asked, pausing the video.

"Sir, I told you about them earlier. The girl in the black dress is Sonam, and the one in white is Sital," Anil said.

"Where are they now? Call them—I want to talk to both," I said.

"Yes, sir, just a minute." Anil took out his phone and dialed. After about 5 minutes, he said,

"Sir, Sonam is coming here soon. But Sital is not picking up her phone."

"Why is she not picking up? Where does she live?"

"She lives in Rose Apartment, near the airport. Maybe she is busy with housework or something."

"Doing housework? Why? Where are her parents?"

"Sir, her parents live in Kochi for a job. She stays here alone in Mumbai for studies."

Just then, the doorbell rang. A constable opened the door—it was Sonam. She looked nervous seeing the police jeep outside.

"Yes, Sonam, come in and sit," I said gently. "Don't worry—we just need your help to find Ajay. Tell me if you know anything that can help."

She sat down and thought for a moment. "Let me think... YES! Sir, there is one boy named Shiva. He doesn't always behave well with Ajay. I think he could do something bad."

"What do you mean by 'not behaving well'? And why do you think he can do something to Ajay?"

"Sir, I don't remember the exact date, but one day when we were sitting in class, Shiva came angrily and shouted at Ajay. He said something like, 'I will show you what real pain is.' It was scary."

"Why did he say that? Was there a fight or something?"

"Ajay didn't tell me the reason after that. He just said Forget it."

"Anil, do you know about this incident?"

"No, sir. Ajay didn't tell me either. But sir, I don't think Shiva can do anything like kidnapping. He is a very introverted type—a quiet boy. He always runs away if a fight starts. He doesn't even talk much."

My phone rang again. I checked—it was Dev calling.

"Sir, I have the call list from Ajay's mobile number."

"Good. What did you find?"

"Sir, the last call Ajay received was from one girl—name saved as SITAL."

"What! What name did you say?"

"Sital, sir."

"Okay, Dev. I will call you back."

I hung up and turned to Anil. "What happened? Did you find something?" Anil asked.

"The last call on Ajay's phone was from Sital. She might know something important. She can help us find him. Where is Sital's house? Let's go there now."

Anil and I quickly left Ajay's house. I told the driver, "Move to the Rose Apartment fast."

After about 15 minutes, we reached the apartment building. It was a nice society with a gate and a guard. We entered, and the guard came forward.

"Yes, sir, what happened? Anything you are looking for?" the guard asked, seeing the police jeep.

"Yes, what is Sital's flat number?" I asked.

"Sir, she is not at home right now."

"Where is she? Did she go out?"

"I don't know exactly, sir. She hasn't come home since two days ago."

"What!" I said, feeling shocked.

"Yes, sir. Around 8:00 PM two days back, she went out wearing a party dress, nice clothes, and makeup. After that, she hasn't come back. Is there any problem?"

My mind was spinning like a wheel. (What is happening? First, Ajay disappears, and now Sital is also missing? Where has she gone?)

CHAPTER SIX

Getting Complicated

"So you are saying that Sital hasn't come home after she went out for the party that night?" I asked the watchman again, making sure I heard correctly.

"Yes, sir," the watchman replied, nodding seriously. "She left around 8:00 PM two days ago, wearing nice party clothes—like a dress and some makeup. After that, no one has seen her come back."

"I want to see her flat right now. Where is the chairman of your society?" I said firmly.

"Come with me, sir," the watchman said and started walking toward the main office.

"Anil, sorry to say this, but you are not allowed to come inside with us. Police rules—you have to wait here only," I told Anil.

He nodded quietly, looking a bit disappointed but understanding. "Okay, sir."

We entered the society's main office. The chairman was sitting behind a desk, looking at some papers. He stood up quickly when he saw the police uniforms.

"What happened, sir? Police in my society... Is everything alright?" he asked, sounding worried.

"Yes, everything is under control. But one boy is missing—his name is Ajay. The last call on his phone was from his friend, who lives here, Sital. And now we have found out that she also hasn't come home since the night he went missing. So we want to check her flat for any clues," I explained.

"Oh! Sital? She is one of the most good and quietest girls in this society. Always polite, pays maintenance on time, no complaints. Come with me—I will show you her flat myself," the chairman said, picking up a spare key.

We took the lift to the 8th floor. "Here, sir—room no. 201, where Sital lives," he said and opened the door carefully.

The flat was small but very neat. Everything was properly arranged—books on the shelf, clothes folded, kitchen clean. It looked like someone who liked order. No signs of any struggle or hurry.

I commanded the constables, "Check everything carefully—drawers, cupboards, bathroom, under the bed. Look for any note, phone, or anything unusual."

I entered her bedroom first. There was a big photo of Sital hanging on the wall—she was smiling brightly, looking happy with friends. Probably a school picture. I checked her almirah—clothes neatly hung, some books and notebooks inside. Nothing related to the case. No letters, no suspicious items.

The constables searched the living room, kitchen, and balcony. One checked her study table—some exam books, pens, and a laptop that was locked. We would need to take that for checking later.

After about 30 minutes of thorough searching, we decided there was nothing obvious. We were about to leave when I turned my attention to the fridge in the kitchen. I looked carefully—there were some magnets, a shopping list, and something written with a marker on the side: a name, "Anshul", with a small heart next to it.

I noted it down mentally. Then we locked the flat and left. Downstairs, Anil was waiting patiently.

"Did you find anything, sir?" he asked as soon as he saw me.

"No, nothing major. The flat is clean and normal. But do you know who Anshul is?" I asked.

"Anshul? Never heard that name before. Why? Did you find something with that name?"

"Leave it for now. Maybe it's nothing. Let's go to your school—I think we can find something there, like talk to teachers or checking with other friends."

"Sir, check the time—it's already 6:30 PM. The school is closed now," Anil said, pointing at his watch.

"Oh yes, you are right. And tomorrow is Sunday, so no school. We will have to go on Monday. Okay then, it's very late—you should go home now. Your mom must be worrying about you a lot."

"Okay, sir. But whenever you need my help, just call me. I will always be there," Anil said seriously.

"Thanks, Anil. You have been very helpful today," I said, and he left on his bike.

I also returned to the station with the constables. As soon as I entered my office, Dev came up.

"Did you find anything, sir? And why did your voice get so loud on the phone when you heard about Sital?" Dev asked curiously.

"No, nothing big at her flat. And about Sital—she is one of Ajay's close friends, the one who was there waiting for the party. Now she has also vanished since that same night."

"What!" Dev said, shocked.

"Yes. Now call Sital's parents in Kochi and ask them to come here as soon as possible. I want to talk to them about her habits, friends, everything."

"Yes, sir," Dev said and went to make the call.

Just then, I got a notification on my phone. I checked—it was a message from the girl I was supposed to meet on Sunday.

"We are meeting tomorrow, but without knowing the timing. Can we decide when we have to meet?" she sent with a laughing emoji.

(No... I have to solve this case first. But how can I say no to her now?)

I was staring at the phone, thinking.

"What happened, sir? You are looking stressed," Dev said, coming back.

"I decided to meet one girl tomorrow—Mom arranged it. But this case is more important to me right now. The problem is, how can I say no to her? My mom will kill me—it's my 7th time rejecting a girl like this."

Dev smiled. "No problem, sir. You go to the meeting. I will handle the case here. It's only a 2-hour meeting, right? I will manage everything."

"But Dev..."

"Please, sir, you go. Anyway, you are getting old for marriage," he joked.

"What! Really?" I said, pretending to be angry. And we both started laughing loudly. It felt good to laugh a little after the tense day.

"Okay then, I will finish the meeting as fast as possible and come back."

"I will also try to find something related to the case and take some leads," Dev promised. Then I left the station and drove to my house. The roads were quieter now in the evening. I opened my door and put the keys on the table. Just then, my phone rang again. I checked— It was my mom.

"Namaste, Maa," I said.

"Namaste, beta. How are you?"

"Fine, Mom. You tell me—how is Papa and Mohit?" I said while taking off my shoes and sitting on the sofa.

"They are also good. Playing chess in the evening, like always. What happened to the girl whose photo I sent you? Did you text her?"

"Yes, Mom. We have decided to meet tomorrow."

"Nice! Go then, beta. I am waiting for your yes this time."

"Maa, I told you before—if her thoughts and mine match, then only I will say yes. It's not just about looks."

"It's fully up to you, beta. Anyway, now tell me—what's happening in Mumbai? Any new cases?"

"I got a new missing person case—two young students now."

"Beta, you know what happened last time with a similar case, so... be careful."

"Yes, Mom, I know. Don't worry—I am good now. Everything is under control."

"Okay. I have to go now—dinner is ready. Take care, beta."

"Bye, Maa."

I opened the chat with the girl and texted back.

"Yes, you are right. We have to decide on the time. So what about 11:00 AM?"

"Okay then, 11:00 done. See you tomorrow!" she replied quickly.

"See you."

I put the phone on the side table, heated some dinner from the fridge—simple roti and sabzi that Priya had made earlier and ate quietly (don't have time to cook anything). Then I took my medicine and got ready for sleep.

But even lying in bed, my mind was only on the case. (Finish this meeting fast tomorrow and get back to the case. Ajay, Sital—where are you guys? What happened that night?)

CHAPTER SEVEN

THE DATE

[2 days after the missing]

I woke up to the alarm and checked my watch—it was 7:30 AM. Sunday morning, but no time to relax. I got out of bed, freshened up quickly—brushed my teeth, took a warm shower to wake myself up properly, and changed into casual clothes. A light blue shirt and jeans, nothing too formal, but neat enough for the meeting. Before leaving, I thought it would be nice to take something for her. Flowers always make a good impression at a first meeting. I drove my car out and stopped in front of a small flower shop near my society. The shop was just opening, with fresh flowers arranged outside.

"Yes, sir, how can I help you?" a middle-aged lady asked with a smile, coming out from behind the counter.

"I want to buy flowers, but I am not very good at choosing the right ones," I admitted.

"No problem, sir. I will help you. Tell me—for what occasion do you want these flowers?"

"Actually, I am going on a date," I said, feeling a bit awkward saying it out loud.

"Oh, for a date! That's sweet. Give me a second—I will make something perfect," she said excitedly.

She went inside and started picking flowers carefully. After about 5 minutes, she came back with a beautiful bouquet—red roses mixed with white lilies and some green leaves. It looked fresh and elegant.

"Here, sir. This will definitely make her happy. And good luck with your date!" she said with a warm smile.

"Thank you so much for your help," I said, paying her and taking the bouquet carefully.

I placed it on the passenger seat and started the long drive to The Food Studio café. Mumbai traffic on Sunday morning was lighter than usual, but it still took time. I reached the place and checked the time—it was 11:20 AM. A bit late, but not too bad.

I entered the café. The interior was really good—soft lighting, wooden tables, nice paintings on the walls, and a pleasant coffee smell in the air. But where was she sitting? I looked around carefully.

I noticed one girl sitting alone at a corner table, waiting for someone. Her back was toward me, so I couldn't see her face properly. She had long hair, and she was checking her phone sometimes. (Looks like she is the one.)

I walked closer and said politely, "Excuse me."

She turned around, and yes—she was exactly the same as in the photo, or I should say much prettier in person. She was wearing a beautiful kurta—pink and white combination, simple but elegant. Her smile was warm.

"Hey, come sit," she said softly.

"Veer," I introduced myself.

"Ruhi," she said, and we both shook hands. Her hand was soft and warm.

"Here, these are for you," I said, giving her the bouquet.

"Wow... they are so beautiful! Thank you so much," she said, her eyes lighting up as she smelled the flowers.

"It's nothing. You look really nice," I said, sitting down opposite her.

"So, tell me something about yourself," I started, trying to make conversation easy.

"Yes, I am a lawyer by profession. I live with my parents here in Mumbai. And yes! I love to travel a lot. I have traveled to many places—almost full north to south India. I like seeing how people live in different areas, their cultures, different clothes, languages, food— Everything feels so new and exciting."

"Do you know about the Nanda Devi temple in Uttarakhand?" I asked, feeling happy that we had something in common.

"Yes! That temple has its main event every 5 years. It's a big festival with the goddess's journey. A very underrated place, not many tourists know about it. The hills there are so peaceful. I think you also like traveling?"

"Yes, a lot. My family is always ready for trips whenever we get free time. In school holidays, we used to go everywhere—hills, beaches, temples. Those are my best memories."

"By the way, how did my mom meet your mom?" I asked curiously.

Ruhi laughed. "Mom was traveling alone on a plane and found a seat next to your mom. They started talking—like old friends—and didn't stop till landing. Then Mom invited your mom for dinner one day and introduced me to her, saying, 'This boy is perfect for my daughter.' After seeing your photos on your mom's phone

"My mom is so talkative, isn't she?" I said.

"Yes!" she said, and we both started laughing loudly.

"No, I am just kidding," she added quickly, still smiling.

"No problem at all. And you said you are a lawyer? Which type—civil, corporate?"

"Criminal cases mostly. And yes, I have won many cases," she said proudly.

"Really? That must be tough—dealing with serious matters every day."

"It is, but when you help someone get justice, it feels worth it."

Just then, the waiter came. "Your order, sir?"

"Order whatever you want, Ruhi," I said.

"Only cold coffee for me, nothing more," she said.

"Same for me," I added.

The waiter noted it down and left.

"Your mom told me you are an IPS officer. So, is there any interesting case you are working on right now?" she asked curiously.

(It's better not to tell her about the missing kids case. Don't want to worry her on the first meet.)

"Nothing much special right now. Just one small thief case we are chasing," I said lightly.

We talked more about favorite travel spots, funny family stories, and food we like—while waiting for the coffee. The cold coffee came—tall glasses with ice cream on top. It tasted perfect on a warm day.

We were enjoying the conversation when suddenly a notification came on my phone. I checked—it was from Dev: "Sital's parents have arrived, sir. When are you coming?"

I felt bad, but sorry, Ruhi, I have to go now. Looks like my team found something about a case," I said honestly.

"No problem at all. I understand—your job is important. And I think we've got to know each other very well in this short time," she said with a smile.

"Yes, definitely. Come, I will drop you home," I offered.

"Sure, thank you."

I paid the bill, and we left the café. I dropped her safely at her place in Chembur—it was on the way anyway. She waved goodbye with the flowers in her hand. And I start moving towards the station.

After some time, I reached the station and checked the time—it was 1:00 PM sharp.

"We were waiting for you only, sir," Dev said as soon as I entered.

"Where are Sital's parents?"

"They are waiting inside your room with their younger daughter."

"Did you tell them about Sital yet?"

"Not yet, sir. Waiting for you."

I entered the room. Sital's parents stood up as soon as they saw me. There were three people—her father, mother, and a small sister who looked about 10 years old.

"Please sit, sir, ma'am. And sorry for making you wait," I said politely.

"What happened, sir? Why did you call us urgently from Kochi? Sital is also not picking up the phone for 2 days. Is everything alright?" her father asked, looking tense.

I noticed the little girl looking curious.

"What's your name, beta?" I asked her softly.

"Angel..." she said shyly.

"Do you like ice cream?"

"Hmm... yes," she replied with a small smile.

"Dev, take her outside and buy her an ice cream—whatever flavor she wants," I said.

"Okay, sir. Come, beta, let's go," Dev said, and they left the room. Now alone with the parents, I took a deep breath.

"Sorry to say this, sir, but your daughter has been missing for 2 days now."

"No!... It's not true," her mother said immediately, tears coming to her eyes.

"It's painful, but it is the reality," I said gently.

"How? When?" her father asked, his voice breaking.

I explained everything calmly—how Ajay called his friends for a party at his house, how he disappeared that night, how Sital was one of the friends waiting outside, and now she hasn't returned home since then either. The CCTV footage, the searches—we told them all.

"What? Ajay is also missing?" her mom asked, shocked.

"Yes, ma'am. Now I want you to tell me everything about Sital—anything that can help us find her."

"What should we tell? She is very innocent. We never got a single complaint from Anyone—teachers, neighbors, no one," her father said.

"Is there any problem she is facing nowadays? Studies, friends, anything?"

"She doesn't talk much on the phone because she is always busy studying for boards. But yes, She has one medical problem from childhood," her father said slowly.

"What problem?"

"She has hemophobia—extreme fear of blood."

"Oh, scared of blood, right? She gets panic attacks if she sees it?"

"Yes, whenever she sees blood—even a small cut—she shouts very loudly and sometimes faints."

"Okay, that's important to know. Is there anyone you think who doesn't like her? Any enemy or problem with someone?"

"I told you already, sir—we never heard a single complaint about her from anyone."

"And yes, there was one name written on her refrigerator—Anshul. Do you know anything about him? Maybe a friend or boyfriend?"

"Anshul? Who is he? We never heard this name from Sital," her father said, looking confused at his wife.

"No, never," her mother added.

"Sir... Ple... please... find her. She is everything for us," her mother said and started crying.

"Please, ma'am, don't cry. I promise I will do my best to find her—and Ajay too. We are putting in all our efforts."

"Thank you so much, sir. We are with you in this," her father said, holding his wife's hand.

They called Angel back, and then they left with their younger daughter. The little girl waved goodbye with her ice cream cone. As soon as they went, Dev came in.

"This case is becoming more complicated, sir," he said.

"Yes, two missing people, connected somehow. We have to find both of them as soon as possible."

I cleaned the whiteboard in my office and started writing all the suspect names and clues.

Ajay — missing first

Sital — last call to Ajay, missing the same night

Shiva — classmate who threatened Ajay once

Anshul — name on fridge, unknown

Tamanna — Ajay's girlfriend, needs to talk

"Hmm... Shiva is a classmate—we have to talk to him tomorrow at school. But we don't get anything about this Anshul. Who is he? We need to find out fast."

I go to my home, eat dinner, and sleep

CHAPTER EIGHT

Classmate

[3 days after the missing]

Today is Monday, and we have a clear plan: go to the school and find out everything possible about Shiva. The case is getting more urgent with every passing hour—Ajay and Sital have been missing for three full days now. I can't let it drag on. I woke up early, around 6:30 AM, feeling the weight of responsibility. After my morning routine—exercise, tea, checking the news on the phone—I got ready properly. Crisp white shirt, polished shoes. As I was picking up my keys to leave, the doorbell rang suddenly. I opened the gate—it was Priya standing there with her usual bag and a bright smile.

"Namaste, sir. I am back for work," she said politely, folding her hands.

"Good to see you back so soon, Priya. Come in. How is your sister, by the way? Everything okay now?" I asked, genuinely concerned.

"She is good now, sir. Walking perfectly, no pain anymore. The doctor said full rest did the magic, and now she is back to normal. Thank you for giving me leave," she replied gratefully.

"Okay then, that's great news. Here are the house keys—everything is as you left it. I might come late today, so don't wait for dinner."

"No problem, sir. I will prepare something and keep it ready."

I locked the door behind her and got into my car. The Mumbai morning was already busy—people heading to work, school buses, street vendors setting up. While driving toward the school, I called Dev on speaker.

"Dev, where are you? Meet me directly at the school gate with two constables. We are going straight to the principal and then the class."

"Yes, sir. We are on the way—will reach in 15 minutes."

"Good. Bring the file with all notes from yesterday, too."

After about 20 minutes of navigating through traffic—stopping at signals—I finally reached the school gate. The campus was massive: tall gates, security checks, wide driveways lined with trees. Students in smart uniforms were entering, some in expensive cars, others on buses.

Dev was already standing outside with the constables, and our police jeep was parked nearby.

"Let's go inside," I said, getting out of my car.

"Yes, sir."

We walked to the main entrance. "Where is the principal's office?" I asked the security guard at the gate.

"Follow me, sir," he said respectfully and started leading us through the beautifully maintained corridors—shiny floors, walls with motivational posters, trophy cabinets full of awards. The school was really pretty big, wasn't it, Dev? Classrooms on both sides, labs visible with modern equipment, even a small auditorium in the distance.

"Yes, sir. This place is huge. Look at that reception area ahead—it looks like a 5-star hotel lobby with sofas and digital screens," Dev whispered, looking around, impressed.

"Sir, this is one of the top elite schools in Mumbai. Very big and famous people's children study here—politicians, actors, businessmen. What are you expecting? Normal private school?" the guard said with a small chuckle.

We reached the principal's office—a big wooden door with a nameplate. Inside, it was air- conditioned (not turned on obviously), spacious with bookshelves, awards, and a large desk.

The principal—a man in his late 50s, wearing a neat suit—stood up immediately after seeing our uniforms.

"Come in, gentlemen. Please have a seat. Tea or coffee?" he offered politely, pointing to comfortable chairs.

"No, thank you. We are here on urgent police work," I said.

"Is there any problem? How can I help you?" he asked, sitting down and looking serious.

"Do you know Ajay and Sital from class 12th?" I started directly.

"Yes, sir. Ajay—a very well-known student. Outgoing, good at sports and studies. Helps organize events. And Sital—a quiet but brilliant girl, always tops in exams. They are both very good seniors. Whenever I see them in assemblies, they give motivational talks to juniors and help with studies.

"Why? What happened to them?" he asked, leaning forward.

"They both have been missing for 3 days now," I said calmly but firmly.

"What! This is terrible... so bad. How can this happen to our students?" he said, genuinely shocked, putting his hand on his forehead.

"Yes, and we need your full help to find them as soon as possible. Time is critical."

"Of course, sir. Whatever you need—full cooperation. Ask anything, I will help in every way possible."

"First, give us permission to talk to the whole class 12th. We need to question the students directly."

"But sir, you cannot tell them openly that Ajay and Sital are missing," he said hesitantly, looking uncomfortable.

"Why not? We need honest answers."

"Sir, please understand—very big lawyers, businessmen, even news reporters and media people's children study here. If any child goes home and talks about this to their parents, our school may face many problems—questions, complaints, and even legal issues. And if this news somehow leaks to the media, our school's reputation could be destroyed completely. Admissions will drop, parents will panic. I don't want that to happen."

"Sir, you are not understanding properly—it's about the children's lives. Their safety is the first priority, not reputation. Sorry, but if we cannot tell the class about the missing, they will take this lightly, hide things, or not tell properly. And I will instruct them strictly not to tell anyone about this case—not even parents or media."

He paused, thinking deeply, rubbing his hands.

"Okay, sir, you are right. Children's lives come first. Reputation can be handled later. I will manage if anything comes up."

He picked up the intercom and called the class teacher of the 12th grade. "Mr. Rahul, come to my office immediately. And send a substitute to cover the class." Soon, the class teacher—a young man in his 30s—came rushing.

"Take these police officers to your classroom. Give them full time to talk to students."

We followed the teacher to the classroom. It was on the first floor—a big, modern room with a projector, comfortable benches. About 40 students were studying quietly. As we entered, Everyone stood up respectfully.

"Sit down, bachho," I said.

"Hello, bachho. How are you all?" I greeted with a smile to ease the tension.

"Good, sir," the whole class replied.

"I am here to talk about a very serious thing, so please cooperate with us fully. Tell me everything honestly, that I ask, okay? And don't be scared—talk freely. No one will punish you for anything."

All the students nodded, looking curious and a bit nervous seeing the police.

"So, Ajay and Sital are missing for the last 3 days..."

"What?", "How can this happen?", "Is it true, sir?" "When?"—the whole class erupted in shocked whispers, questions flying everywhere. Some girls looked scared, and boys exchanged glances.

"Keep quiet, everybody! No talking! First listen to sir properly," the class teacher shouted from the door, and the class became pin-drop silent again.

"Thank you. So, your two friends are missing, and we need your help to find them as soon as possible. Any small information can save their lives."

"Sir, ask whatever you want. We will give you all the answers truthfully," one boy from the front. Bench said confidently, and others nodded.

"Okay then. First question—has Ajay or Sital messaged, called, or sent anything to anyone here in the last few days? Any unusual contact?"

Everyone stayed silent, looking at each other's faces, shaking their heads slowly. No one spoke up.

"Okay, no problem. Next— is there someone in the class or school who doesn't talk much or doesn't behave well with these two? Anyone who had a fight, argument, or problem with Ajay or Sital?"

Again, silence for a few minutes. Students were thinking hard, some looking down.

Then I noticed two girls in the back row whispering urgently about something, glancing around nervously.

"Hey, you two in the back—stand up please. Tell me what happened. What were you whispering? Do you know someone like that?" I pointed directly.

One girl stood up hesitantly, her friend pushing her lightly.

"Yes, sir... There is one boy, Shiva. He doesn't like these two much."

(Oh yes, Shiva—I remembered Sonam's mention about the threat and now this.)

"Where is he now? Is he in class?" I asked, looking around.

"No, sir. He has been absent for the last 2-3 days," she said.

"Why doesn't he like them? What happened between them?"

"Sir, actually, Shiva comes from a very small place, a poor family, not like most of us. So no one talks to him much in school. He stays alone, eats alone, and studies alone. One day, after school was over, he was going back home on his old bicycle. Ajay was playing with friends and accidentally threw an empty cold drink can—it hit Shiva on the head, and he lost balance, fell down hard on the road. Everyone around started laughing loudly, including Sital, who was there. Shiva got hurt—physically and more in his heart, embarrassed in front of everyone. Since that day, he stopped talking to them completely. Avoids them." The girl sat down, looking sorry.

"So bad behavior. In school, everyone is equal—no matter rich or poor, from a slum or a bungalow. You all have to treat each other normally, with respect. Making fun of someone like that is wrong," I said strictly, looking at the whole class.

"Sorry, sir," all students said together, many with heads down in shame. Just then, the bell rang loudly for the next period.

"Okay then, bachho. Thank you for your time. If anyone remembers anything more or finds any clue about Ajay or Sital—any message, sighting, anything—don't tell anyone else. Come directly to me or any police station. And very important—don't tell anyone about this conversation today—not friends outside class, not your parents, no one—because if news spreads, it will make it harder for us to find them safely."

"Okay, sir, we all understand. We promise," one boy said from the front, and the whole class nodded seriously.

"Thank you all for your cooperation. Study well," I said, and we left the room with the teacher taking us back.

"Let's go to the principal's office again. We need full details about Shiva now," I told Dev outside.

"Yes, sir."

We entered the principal's office once more. He was waiting anxiously.

"Yes, sir? Did you find something useful?" he asked as we sat.

"Yes. I want everything about Shiva—full name, address, parents' details, contact numbers, everything."

"Shiva...? Oh, Shiva Patil. He is a very introverted type of boy. Quiet, no friends really, but studies very well, always in the top 5. Came from a slum area in Dharavi."

"Slum area? After seeing your school—big buildings, high facilities—I think the fees are very high. Expensive here," Dev said, surprised.

"Yes, annual fees are in lakhs— one of the most expensive in Mumbai."

"So how can a boy from a slum area afford this? Family business or something?" Dev asked.

"No. Scholarship," I guessed.

"Yes, exactly right," the principal confirmed. "Every year, our school conducts a big scholarship test—open to all children in the city, even from government or small schools. Thousands participate. Toppers qualify, and then from them, 3 lucky students get a 100% fee waiver—including books, uniform—by a lucky draw. Shiva topped the exam two years ago and won the scholarship. A very bright and hardworking boy. His family is poor—father works as a laborer, mother at home."

"Nice concept—really good. Gives a chance to talented kids who deserve it," Dev said appreciatively.

"Yes, we are proud of it. Helps diversity too."

"Give me his full address and contact details," I said.

"Give me a second—let me pull up the records," the principal said and started typing on his computer, then calling the admin office for the file.

After about 10 minutes of waiting—printing forms, checking numbers—he handed me a printed sheet.

"Here it is—full address in Dharavi, father's name and mobile, everything. You can take a photo or note down."

"Thanks, sir, for all your help today. You cooperated fully."

"No mention, sir. If there is anything else I can do—more records, call parents, anything— tell me without any hesitation. And yes, please find our students as soon as possible. They are good kids—the future of the country."

"Okay, sir. We will do our best," I promised, standing up.

Then we left the school, walking back to the jeep under the hot sun. As soon as we sat inside, Dev turned to me excitedly.

"Sir, I think Shiva is the one who did this to them. See the timing—he threatened Ajay once, got humiliated by both, and now he is also absent from the exact day those two went missing. Too many coincidences."

"Maybe. Everything points toward him right now. Introvert, hurt ego, opportunity. Let's go to his home right away and clear all things—talk to him and his family."

"Yes, sir. Driver, start—next stop Dharavi, the address here."

CHAPTER NINE

HATRED AND CLUES

"Let's go... wait! There is a problem," I said suddenly as we were about to leave the school premises and head to the jeep.

"What, sir?" Dev asked, stopping in his tracks.

"If we go to that slum area in Dharavi wearing these police uniforms, everyone will notice us immediately. People will gather around, asking questions, wanting to know what's happening. There's a big chance that Shiva gets alerted and runs away before we even reach his house. You all go change into plain clothes—casual shirts and pants."

"Yes, sir. Smart thinking. We will be right back in 5 minutes," Dev said, and he, along with the Constables, hurried to the jeep to grab spare clothes we always keep for undercover work.

While waiting, I stood outside the school gate, watching the world go by. Parents were picking up younger kids, some walking hand-in-hand. I saw one man—a father—holding his little son's hand tightly, swinging it playfully as they walked toward an ice cream cart nearby.

The boy was laughing, pointing at flavors.

(How time passes so fast. I remember when I was a child, my father used to take me just like this after school—holding my hand, buying kulfi or ice cream from the street vendor. Those simple joys. This big school also reminds me of our old school days in Uttarakhand. Small building, but full of life. How our teacher, Mr. Harsh, always cracked those silly jokes in class—everyone would burst out laughing, even during serious lessons. What golden days those were—carefree, playing in the hills after school, no worries about cases or missing people.)

After about 10 minutes, Dev and the other constables came back, now in casual shirts—plain t-shirts, jeans, and pants. No uniforms, no badges visible. They looked like normal young men.

"We are ready, sir. Let's go," Dev said.

I entered my car and gave instructions through the window. "Follow me closely. No sirens, no rushing. We go quietly."

We started the drive. Mumbai traffic was building up—lunch hour approaching. After about 20 minutes of navigating narrow roads, flyovers, and crowded signals, we finally reached the entrance of Dharavi—one of Asia's largest slum areas. The streets turned narrow instantly—houses built very close to each other, barely space for one car to pass. Clothes hanging on lines overhead, kids playing everywhere, smells of street food mixing in the air.

We parked the vehicles at a safer spot outside the main lanes—we couldn't take the cars deeper. Now on foot.

I spotted three small children playing nearby, rolling old tyres with sticks like a game. I called them over gently. "Hey, bachho, come here for a minute."

They stopped and came closer, curious but cautious.

"What happened? Don't waste our time—we are playing," one older kid said with an arrogant tone, hands on his hips.

"Hey, watch your tone," Dev said sternly.

"Leave it, Dev. They are only kids," I said calmly. "So, what's your name, beta?" I asked the arrogant one with a smile.

"Why should I tell you? Just say what you want, or we are going back to play," he replied.

"We just want to know which one is Shiva's house. Shiva bhaiya from the big school."

The kids looked at each other. The arrogant one thought for a second.

"Hmm... Shiva bhaiya? Go straight from here, then take the left where you see the blue water pipe. After that, where you see a pink house with flowers outside, take the right turn. Then again straight—second last house with brown color walls and a black water tank on the roof. That's his."

"Thanks a lot for the help, champions," I said, patting one on the shoulder. We followed the boy's instructions carefully—turning through the maze-like narrow lanes, avoiding puddles, ducks walking around, people staring but not interfering much. Finally, after the right turn, I saw it—the house matching exactly: brown faded walls, small door, black tank on the tin roof.

"Oh, here it is," Dev whispered.

I knocked on the thin wooden door gently. "Anyone home?"

"Coming!" a woman's voice came from inside.

After a minute, the door opened. A lady in her 40s, wearing a simple red saree, wiping her hands on it—probably cooking.

"Yes? Who are you?" she asked politely.

"Hello, ma'am. I am Veer, and these are my colleagues... (I should tell her we are from school. If I say police officer now, she will panic immediately, maybe hide Shiva or make excuses to save her son.) We are from your son's school. Principal Sir sent us for some urgent documents and to check on Shiva."

"Oh! School teachers? Come inside then, please. Shiva is bathing right now—he will come in a few minutes," she said, opening the door wider with a relieved smile.

"No problem, ma'am. We will wait for him," I said, and we decided to move inside carefully.

The house was very small—one main room serving as living, kitchen, and bedroom is on the roof, I think. Light was not coming properly inside, through a small window high up. Walls are dull and patchy, but surprisingly clean. Floor swept neatly.

My eyes went to one corner—a small shelf full of medals, trophies, and certificates shining even in dim light.

"Tea or coffee, sir?" the lady offered hospitably, going toward the stove.

"Sorry, ma'am, we already drank coffee before coming here. Thank you," I said.

"By the way, there are so many medals and trophies here—very impressive," I pointed to the shelf.

"These all are Shiva's," she said proudly, her face lighting up. "He is a very smart boy.

Always brings something from school—top in class, quiz winner, scholarship, everything. We are poor, but he studies so hard day and night."

"I see. That's really good," I said, glancing at the awards—math olympiad, science fair, best student.

We waited quietly for about 10 minutes, making small talk about school. Then the curtain moved, and Shiva finally entered the room.

He was tall for his age—around 5'10"—with long, messy hair, pimples on his face, thin build. Wearing a simple black shirt and black pants, with a towel around the neck.

"Who are they, Mom?" he asked, looking at us suspiciously.

"They are from your school only. You don't know? Principals sent them," his mom said innocently.

"Sorry, sir, but I didn't recognize you. Are you new teachers?" Shiva asked politely but cautiously.

"Principal sir sent us here for some important documents and verification. Can we talk to you alone for a minute?" I said calmly.

"Okay... let's move outside then," he agreed, still confused.

We stepped out into the narrow lane—away from the door so his mom couldn't hear.

"Yes, sir, what do you want to ask me?" he said.

I came close to him, lowered my voice, and said firmly, "Listen carefully, Shiva. I am not from your school. I am Inspector Veer Singh from the police. I am here to take you to the police station for questioning. Don't even think about running or shouting—my officers are around. You understand?"

His face went pale instantly. "But sir... I didn't do anything wrong!"

"Keep quiet for now. Just go inside, tell your mother you are going with us for some school work, and come peacefully."

He nodded slowly, scared. Went inside, told his mom something about "school project help." She smiled and said

Okay.

We started walking back through the lanes toward where we parked the cars. Shiva in the middle, Dev on one side.

"Get inside the jeep," Dev said, opening the door. We all got in, and the vehicles moved toward the police station—no drama, no attention. Back at the station, in the interrogation room.

"Dev, take his phone first. Check everything—messages, calls, photos. See if anything is related to the case," I instructed.

"Yes, sir," Shiva said quietly, looking down.

"First of all, thank you, sir. You didn't tell my mother that you are taking me to the police station," he said softly, gratefully.

"It's okay. We didn't want to worry her unnecessarily. Now tell me straight—where are Ajay and Sital?"

"In their houses, I think. I really don't know, sir," he replied, confused.

"By the way, why have you not been coming to school for 3 days?"

"I have had viral fever for 3 days, sir. Body pain, headache—that's why I couldn't go to school. Mom can tell you."

Dev came back with the phone.

"Sorry to interrupt, sir, but see what I found. He chatted with one guy named Bablu, 2 days before the missing. Look at this conversation yourself."

I took the phone from Dev and started reading the messages carefully.

Shiva: Hey, bro, I need help urgently.

Bablu: What happened? What kind of help?

Shiva: It's kind of a risky job...

Bablu: Just tell me directly. You know I can do anything for you.

Shiva: You have to kidnap one boy from our school for a short time.

Bablu: Sorry, bro, you know I stopped doing kidnapping stuff anymore. Too much risk.

Shiva: Please, bro, I will give you a good amount. It's a request from the younger brother to the older brother. I don't want any harm to him—you just have to scare him a bit and make him say sorry to me in front of the whole school. Nothing more, I promise.

Bablu: Hmm.... Okay then, it's a deal—for you only.

Shiva: Thank you so much, bro! His name is Ajay. Let's meet at our secret place tonight, and there I will give you his full details—photo, address, routine.

Bablu: You are like my real brother—don't thank me. See you at night at our usual place.

"What is this, Shiva? You told someone to kidnap Ajay?" I asked, showing him the screen. He looked at the messages, face turning red, and suddenly started crying—tears rolling down.

"Sir... you know how it feels when the whole school makes fun of you, laughs at you openly? After that incident, everyone started teasing me daily—calling names, mimicking my fall. Even my only friend in school came one day and said that because of me, others make fun of him too, and he broke the friendship. I was completely alone. Anger built up, and one day I said those words to Ajay in anger. But I didn't mean real kidnapping... just wanted to scare him so he says sorry publicly and stops others."

"But you messaged about kidnapping!"

"I... I was angry, sir. But Bablu is like my brother—he lives nearby. I thought he would just act, pretend... not real.

But after sending details, I felt bad and told him the next day to cancel. He said Okay."

"We will check that. But right now, things look very serious." Shiva kept crying quietly.

"Shiva, you are under arrest for conspiracy to kidnap Ajay, and are possibly connected to Sital's disappearance, too. We will investigate fully."

CHAPTER TEN

MOTHERS LOVE

"Sir, please don't arrest me. I beg you," Shiva pleaded again, his voice full of fear, tears streaming. down his cheeks, hands folded in front of him like praying.

"Stop crying now and tell me exactly where Sital and Ajay are," I said sternly, trying to keep my voice calm but firm in the dimly lit interrogation room.

"Sir, I swear on my mother—I really don't know about them. I have no idea where they are or what happened?" he repeated, wiping his face with his sleeve.

"And what about these messages on your phone? Clear proof," I pointed out, pushing the phone. screen toward him again.

"It's correct, sir... I admit that I told Bablu to kidnap Ajay. But that plan was for Sunday, two days ago. later. I don't know who took him before us on that Friday night when he disappeared. And as you can see clearly in the chats, I mentioned only Ajay—not Sital once. She has nothing to do with my anger or plan."

"Stop making up stories, Shiva. Everything is against you—tell us the full truth. It's all over now." Dev said from the corner, his tone serious.

"Sir... please, please believe me. I really don't know anything more," Shiva said, looking down, shoulders shaking.

"Where is Bablu right now? His location?" I asked, shifting the question.

"I don't know exactly, sir. I think he is not even in Mumbai anymore. He never has a fixed place—he moves from city to city for his... jobs."

"Not in Mumbai? Okay then—call him immediately. I want to talk to him myself. Put the phone on. speaker mode," I ordered.

"Yes, sir... give me a second," Shiva said nervously, dialing the number with trembling fingers.

(Come on, Bablu, pick up the phone. We need answers.)

The call rang several times—tense moments—then finally connected.

"Hello..." a deep, rough voice answered from the other side, sounding cautious.

"Keep talking naturally," I whispered very low to Shiva, signaling him to continue.

"Yes, brother, how are you? Long time," Shiva said, forcing a normal tone.

"Good, bro. You okay? Anything you want to ask or need?" Bablu replied casually.

"Not really. Just called to check. Let's meet at our usual secret place soon—like old times."

"No, can't do, brother. I am not in Mumbai right now—left the city."

"Where are you then? Tell me, we can plan."

"Sorry, can't share the exact location over the phone. But yeah, I am up in Dehradun—hiding from someone. police trouble, old case."

"What! Hiding from the police again? What did you do this time?

"That boy.... Leave it, bro, can't discuss details—too risky. And listen, I am destroying everything —phone, SIM cards, all contacts. Going off-grid completely. So I won't be in. connection for like 2-3 months at least, okay? Take care of yourself. Now I really have to go—bye."

"Wait... hello?" Shiva tried, but the line had already disconnected. Dead tone. We all sat silent for a second.

"That boy... I don't know why, sir, but I have a strong feeling that Bablu knows exactly where Ajay and Sital are—or at least involved somehow," Dev said, breaking the silence.

"Same here, Dev. The timing, the hiding, mentioning Dehradun specifically—too suspicious. Shiva, do you have any photos of Bablu? Even an old one or with someone?"

"No, sir. He always strictly refuses to click photos—says in his line of work, no records, no evidence."

"Dev, arrange a police sketch artist immediately. We need a detailed composite of Bablu. on Shiva's description."

"Sir, it's almost 10 PM now. No artist will come at this late hour."

"Oh yes, you are right. Then first thing tomorrow morning—no delay."

"Can I go home now, sir? Please. My mom will be worried," Shiva asked, looking exhausted.

"Yes, go. But you must report here tomorrow morning sharp—at 8 AM. And don't even think about running away or contacting Bablu to tip him off."

"Sir, I swear again—my only purpose was to scare Ajay a little, make him apologize publicly. Nothing more harmful. And I didn't kidnap him—you saw the chats, plan was later. I am fully with you, sir. I want this solved too."

"Good attitude. Now go home safely."

Shiva stood up slowly, thanked us quietly, and left the station.

"You also look too tired, sir—eyes red," Dev said as we locked the room.

"Yeah, very long day—too much running around. I need proper sleep. See you tomorrow, bright and early, Dev."

"Okay, sir. Good night. Drive safe."

I drove home through the quiet late-night Mumbai streets—few vehicles, cool breeze. Reached home, changed into comfortable clothes quickly, took my medicine pills, and fell into a deep sleep almost immediately.

Next day [4 days after the missing]

I woke up at my regular time—7:00 AM sharp. The case pressure was there, but the body felt rested. Freshened up—shower, shave—made a quick breakfast: boiled eggs, bread, toast, strong tea. Changed into a fresh uniform and drove to the station, mind already planning the day. Dev was standing outside the station gate, looking ready with files.

"Good morning, sir!" he greeted energetically.

"Good morning, Dev. Where is the artist? And has Shiva come?"

"They are both inside the room, sir. The artist is taking his time to get every detail right from Shiva."

"Good. Pack your bags quickly—we are going to Dehradun today itself to catch Bablu. coordinating with local Dehradun police."

"Right now, sir? So sudden?"

"Dev, we don't have time to waste. Five days have already gone by. I promised Ajay's and Sital's parents personally that I will bring their children back safe—you were there, you know that. Bablu mentioned Dehradun while 'hiding'—we can't ignore that lead."

"Yes, sir, absolutely. I know how much it means. But flights are cancelled for 2 days for Dehradun, we have to go by train, it will take 1 day, but only option left, Raghu ji!" Dev called the Constable nearby. "Urgently book 2 train tickets—Mumbai to Dehradun. Fastest available today."

I entered the station and went straight to the sketch artist. Shiva was sitting with the artist, describing features carefully—nose shape, eyes, scars.

"Okay, that's it. Anything else you remember? Hair style, marks?" the artist asked one last time.

"No, that's everything about his face—build, height too," Shiva confirmed.

"Done, sir. Here is your criminal sketch," the artist said proudly, handing over the detailed drawing.

I examined it closely: long, untied hair, one earring in the left ear, a small black mole below the left eye, a rough stubble beard, a sharp jawline, around 25-30 age look.

"Is this sketch matching perfectly, Shiva? Any change needed?"

"Yes, sir—almost 100% exact. That's Bablu."

"Excellent. Now you can go home," I told the artist.

"Okay, sir. If you need any changes or another version, call me anytime," he said, packing his tools and leaving.

"Can I also go now, sir?" Shiva asked hopefully.

"Okay, go. But remember strictly—if any call, message, or anything from Bablu, contact us directly. No delays, no hiding."

"Sure, sir. I promise—I will inform immediately." Shiva left, looking serious.

After about 40 minutes, Dev came rushing in with a small travel bag slung over his shoulder.

"Yes, sir—tickets booked! The train leaves at 10 AM. Ready to go?"

"Okay, good. Let's move."

"But sir, where is your bag? Clothes, things for days?"

"I don't need one at all."

"Why, sir?" Dev asked, puzzled.

"Because I am from Dehradun originally—my family home is there. All my stuff, clothes—everything is at home."

"Oh, really! I had no idea. Sir, from hills—like fresh air, mountains, now you have to treat"

"Ok, I will treat you to local dinner—garhwali food, momos, everything."

"Thank you so much, sir! Can't wait."

"Kunal, drop us at the railway station—fast but safe."

The drive took only 35 minutes—morning traffic light on.. We reached the bustling station—crowds everywhere, announcements echoing, the smell of food stalls.

"What is the exact timing of our train?" I asked.

"It's at 10 AM sharp, sir. We have about 40 minutes to spare." Dev confirmed

"I hate waiting around in stations—too noisy."

"Tea, sir? The best way to pass the time. Strong cutting chai."

"Okay, fine. Let's go find a good stall."

We walked toward a popular tea shop outside the platform area. Only a 3-minute walk.

"We also had a small tea shop like this in our town when I was young," Dev said nostalgically, going towards the shop.

"Oh, really? So you started from a tea seller's family to a police officer—quite a journey, inspiring."

"Thank you, sir. I always remember those old days. and my father sells tea all day—from early morning to late evening. Customers coming, going. Then in the evening, I would go wash the plates at the end. Come home tired, but then study all night under one bulb for the police entrance exams. Sir, those were really hard days—body aching, but mind strong."

"But interestingly, sir, I never dreamed of becoming a police officer as a child."

"What, really? Then what?"

"Yes, sir. Kid me had no big dreams—just play cricket, roam with friends, no cares. But one day, returning home from playing, I overheard my mother crying in the kitchen. She was removing her. Last gold kangan (bangles) and giving to father, saying with tears, 'This is the last valuable thing I have now. Sell these and pay the school fees somehow. I don't want my children to suffer the same poverty and struggles that I faced in my childhood—no food some days, no books.' Her words hit me like arrows straight in the heart. My parents sacrificed everything—dreams, Comfort—for us, and I was wasting time bunking classes for fun. NO MORE! From that exact day, I decided—one aim only: become something big, make them proud, change family fate. I researched jobs and found a police officer—one of the most respected, powerful, and helpful to society. Started preparation seriously."

"Wow, Dev—that's truly motivating. So when did you find time to study with all the work?"

"Daytime—help mom-dad at the tea stall: serve customers, make chai perfectly, clean. Evening—wash plates for money. Night—study under dim light till late. Sleep less, but focus. I just wanted one thing: parents seeing me in a police uniform, saluting proudly."

I nodded, impressed by his determination.

"I gave the tough exam, but wasn't confident about the result. Some days later, I was sitting at our tea shop counter suddenly heard a loud collapsing sound outside. Ran out—saw my father fallen on the ground, holding their chest, face pale. Shouted for help, carried him to the nearest hospital, somehow. The doctor said massive heart attack—trying best to save... After one long hour waiting outside, the doctor came out shaking his head: Sorry, we couldn't save him..." Dev paused, voice cracking, eyes turning red again. "My whole body froze—like a statue. All sounds disappeared. I just saw my mother collapsing, crying, and our relatives were sad. Suddenly, my best friend came running, shouting—You cracked the exam! Selected for police training!" He wiped his eyes quickly.

"Why did this happen to me, sir? I did nothing wrong ever. Only one dream—Papa holding my police cap, smiling proudly on passing out day..."

I had no words. Just patted his back gently, letting emotion pass.

"Oh, so sorry, sir. I never shared this full story with anyone before—that's why emotions. overflowed. Couldn't control."

"Oh no, Dev—it's completely okay. You kept it bottled up inside for years. Sharing helps sometimes. Feels lighter."

"Thank you for listening, sir."

(And then, as usual, after such emotional deep talks, about 2 minutes of comfortable silence.)

"And any little brothers or sisters?" I asked to break the silence lightly.

"Oh yes—one younger sister. She turned 22 this year. The whole family is finding a good boy for her marriage soon—arranged, with a horoscope match, everything."

"Oh, nice. Wish she finds a loving, responsible husband."

"See, we are finally at the tea shop properly."

We sat on empty plastic stools. Dev signaled the chaiwala—two special cutting chai. Hot steaming tea arrived in small glasses—perfect ginger-cardamom flavor. We sipped slowly, talked lighter topics—favorite movies, Mumbai traffic jokes—for the next 15 minutes.

"It's almost time, sir. Let's head back to the platform," Dev said, checking phone time.

"Yes, you are right. The train will be there at any minute."

We paid and walked back just as the announcement came for our train boarding. After 2 minutes, the long train arrived—engines humming, doors opening. We found our reserved AC seats comfortably, and kept our bags overhead. Once settled, and train started moving.

"Sorry, sir—I forgot to ask yesterday about your date. How did it go? Everything good?" Dev asked curiously.

"Perfect, actually. We talked so much—flowed naturally. Good thing: we both liked each other a lot. Same interests."

"Oh, great news! So what does she do?"

"She is a criminal lawyer—handles court cases."

"So one catches criminals, the other fights for justice in court—what a perfect match made!" Dev joked.

We both started laughing heartily.

"Kinda true. But first, she has to say yes to the next steps—marriage."

"Hmm, I think if everything matches, she will definitely say yes." Just then, Dev's phone rang loudly.

"Yes, Ma... what are you doing now?... I am good, healthy... yes, going outstation to

Dehradun With Sir for an important case... You want something from there? Woolen shawl for winter? Okay, will bring the best one... bye, love you, Ma." He disconnected, smiling.

"My mother—always worrying."

"Every mother is the same—wants her child safe, no problems. Especially when sons do risky jobs like ours—chases, dangers."

"True, sir. Very true."

"Now just think about Ajay's mother and Sital's mother—how they must be feeling right now, sleepless nights, not knowing if children are safe or..."

"Yes, sir. Breaks heart. We have to find them at any cost. First priority—catch this Bablu, make him talk."

"Our train reaches Dehradun around 11:00 PM tomorrow—a full-day journey. Enough time to rest the body properly, because after reaching, I don't think we will have time to relax even a minute."

"You are right, sir. Full action from there."

We both reclined seats, put on the blankets provided, and slept peacefully as the train sped through the night.

(After all the long journey—scenery changing from urban to rural plains to finally green. Hills—we finally reached Dehradun railway station late at night. The whole 5th day is gone in travelling.

"Brr... It's really cold here!" Dev said, shivering as we stepped on the platform, rubbing his hands.

"Welcome to Dehradun, Dev—hill station winter," I said, breathing the crisp, fresh mountain air. Felt instantly like home—memories flooding.

We took a prepaid cab from outside—night roads quiet, pine trees visible in headlights. After a peaceful 30-minute ride, we reached my family's house, ancestral home in a calm. residential area, with front garden, big iron gate, and lights on.

"Wow, sir. Beautiful house—peaceful location. I also dream of a house like this one day," Dev said admiringly.

"This place is everything for my father—or I can say for my whole family. Childhood, memories, roots—all here." I pressed the doorbell twice—our old signal.

After 2 minutes, the porch light came on, door opened slowly.

"Who is this at this late hour..." Mom said, peering out, then saw my face.

"SURPRISE, Ma!" I said with a big grin, opening my arms.

"VEER! My son—is this really you? What a pleasant surprise! Come inside fast—cold outside. I can't believe you came without informing. And who is this young man with you?"

"He is Dev, Mom—my trusted sub-inspector. We are solving an urgent case together, and it's connected here, so he will stay with us for some days."

"Namaskar, ma'am," Dev said respectfully, touching her feet.

"Namaskar, beta. Long life and success. Come in both—no hotel talk. Stay here as many days as needed. Treat it like your own house, only," Mom said warmly, blessing Dev and hugging me tightly.

"Thank you so much, ma'am."

"Where are Papa and Mohit?" I asked, entering the familiar living room—same furniture, family photos on the walls.

"They are sleeping upstairs—tired from the day. You both must also be exhausted from the journey. Freshen up, have warm milk, then sleep. We will talk about everything tomorrow morning properly."

"No worries, Ma. It's too late already—we don't want to disturb. We will meet them fresh in the morning. Now Dev and I are going to my old room. Good night, love you."

"Good night, my beta. So happy you came home."

We went upstairs to my childhood room—posters still there, bookshelves, a window overlooking hills. Dev took the guest bed.

Finally, home—and ready for the chase starting tomorrow.

CHAPTER ELEVEN

SECRET MEETING

[6 days after the missing]

Waking up in my own childhood house is always so relaxing—the familiar creak of the wooden bed, the cool hill air coming through the window, birds chirping outside in the pine trees. No Mumbai noise, no traffic horns. Just peace. I stretched, feeling refreshed after a good sleep.

As I sat up, Dev—who was on the guest bed—was already awake, folding his blanket neatly.

"Good morning, sir," he said with a smile.

"Good morning, Dev. Slept well? Let's get ready—today we have to report to the local police station and start the hunt properly."

"Yes, sir, I know. The bed was comfortable, air fresh—best sleep in days. I am ready in 5 minutes."

We both freshened up quickly—bath in the attached bathroom with hot water from the geyser, changed into casual but professional clothes (no uniforms to avoid attention yet).

We stepped out of the room and went downstairs. The smell of fresh parathas and tea was already filling the house. Dad and my brother Mohit (Golu, as we call him) were sitting at the dining table, reading the newspaper and scrolling phone. Mom was in the kitchen, busy cooking. I walked toward them quietly from behind.

"Namaskar, Papa," I said, bending to touch his feet respectfully. Dev followed me exactly, touching my feet too.

"Bless you, beta. Long life, success," Papa said, putting his hand on my head. Then to Dev,

"Bless you, too, son."

"How are you, Veer? You came without telling anyone—sudden visit," Papa said, folding the newspaper.

"Yes, actually, we are working on a very urgent case, Papa. The lead brought us here suddenly—no time to inform."

"No problem at all. This is your house only—come anytime, stay as long as needed," he said warmly, taking a sip of his hot tea.

"And Golu, how are you? Still playing only cricket all day, or studying also sometimes?" I teased my younger brother, who was sitting quietly, looking a bit shy with the guests.

"Nothing much, Bhaiya. Winter vacation just started, so making a timetable with friends— cricket in the morning, studies evening," he replied with a smile.

"Good, have fun, but don't forget books completely. And Papa, he is..."

"Dev, right? Mom told us everything last night after you slept. Welcome, beta—sit, breakfast almost ready," Papa said kindly.

"No, Dad, actually it's a very important case—we have to rush to the local station now," I replied politely.

"Beta, at least eat something... I made aloo parathas—your favourite," Mom called from the kitchen, coming out with a plate.

"No, Mom, thank you so much. We will eat later. And yes, I think we will be late tonight, so you all can sleep early. Put the extra key under the doormat like always."

"Okay, beta, but don't be too late. I am making your most favourite Mom special for dinner— rajma chawal, with butter and your favourite sweet," she said, hugging me quickly.

"Alright, Mom—sounds delicious. Now, please, can we go? We are here for a very important case—can't delay."

I hugged Mom once more, waved to Papa and Golu, and left the house with Dev. We walked down the quiet colony road—fresh morning air, people doing yoga in parks, school kids on cycles. After a walk, we took an auto rickshaw from the stand.

"Bhai, police station—fast," I told the driver.

It took almost 45 minutes to reach—winding hill roads, some traffic in market areas.

"Wow, sir—the station looks so clean and green. Flowers outside, painted nicely," Dev said as we got down.

"It's Uttarakhand, Dev—everything cleaner, calmer than Mumbai," I said proudly.

We entered the station compound—a small but organised building, the Uttarakhand Police board shining.

"Yes, how can I help you?" a young constable at the reception desk asked.

"I am Inspector Veer Singh, and this is Sub-Inspector Dev—we are here from Mumbai Police."

"Jai Hind, sir!" he said, standing up straight and giving a sharp salute.

"Jai Hind," I replied.

"Give me a minute, sir—I will call Inspector Sir immediately." He went inside a cabin and signalled us to come in.

We entered the room—a simple office, files neat, a heater running.

"Jai Hind, sir. Welcome to Dehradun. Tell me—how can I help you?" the local Inspector—a tall man in his 40s, nameplate reading Inspector Rawat—asked respectfully.

"Jai Hind. We are here regarding a serious missing persons case from Mumbai—two teenagers. We have a strong tip that the main suspect is hiding here in Dehradun."

"Can you tell me his name or show a sketch if possible?"

"Yes, his name is Bablu—local criminal type. Here is his police sketch," I said, taking out my phone and showing the detailed drawing from yesterday.

Inspector Rawat looked carefully, then showed it to the constable Kelash.

"Oh yes! I know this face very well. Kelash, do you remember?" he said.

"Yes, sir—Bablu, right. Local goon. We have recent information that he and his gang of 4-6 people are involved in supplying drugs, mostly to college students, parties, and even some schools. We are also searching for him actively. Last tip was he sells in clubs—both legal and illegal ones."

"So first, we have to start a thorough investigation in all clubs as much as possible—to know anything about this Bablu or his drug gang operations," I said.

"You are right, sir. It's 11:00 AM now—we have 8-9 hours before clubs start filling up in the evening."

"Best plan—make multiple teams. Divide the list of all known clubs in the city. Cover maximum ground fast," I suggested.

"Sir, take our jeep with 2-3 more constables. I will coordinate other teams," Inspector Rawat offered.

(We quickly divided all known clubs—about 20 legal and some illegal tips—into routes for teams. Everyone is ready to go.)

"Let's go, sir. All the best—stay in touch on the radio," Rawat said, saluting.

We entered the jeep—me, Dev, the driver, and two local constables.

"Driver, move to our first club on the list," I instructed.

"Sir, do you think Bablu or his drug gang will come to clubs today itself?" Dev asked doubtfully.

"Anything is possible, Dev. Criminals get bold sometimes. Or what if even one club worker knows about Bablu—his hideout, contacts?"

It took almost 30 minutes to reach the first one, through a busy market, up some slopes. "BLUE FISH—what a funny name for a club," Dev said, reading the neon sign—still off in daytime.

We entered—dim lights even day, music system testing, 5-6 workers cleaning tables, arranging bar.

"Yes, sir, how can I help you?" a middle-aged man in a shirt approached.

"Who are you? We want to talk to the manager," I said authoritatively.

"I am the manager only, sir. Tell me—what can I do for you?" "We are police—working on a serious case. Do you know or recognise this man?" I showed the sketch clearly.

"Sir, this is a club—hundreds of new people come daily, parties every night. How should I remember one face? Let me ask my workers and staff," he said cooperatively. He showed the sketch to all—bartenders, waiters, cleaners, DJ. After 5 minutes of checking, "No, sir—no one recognises him. Sorry."

We thanked and moved to the next clubs on the list—same routine: enter, ask the manager, show the sketch to all staff, and question if any suspicious activities have recently occurred. We searched many clubs—one after another: flashy ones in mall areas, small underground types in basements, even some lounge bars. Asked everyone—owners, bouncers, regular suppliers. But we found nothing—no recognition, no tips about Bablu. Hours passed—lunch quick roadside Maggi in between.

"Sir, it's almost evening time—clubs will start opening and filling soon," Dev said, checking his watch around 6 PM.

"Yes, Dev, but what can we do? No one knows about Bablu or has seen him recently. Call other teams—ask if they found something or not. Dev nodded and moved aside for a radio call—contacting each team.

(BABLU, where are you hiding? This case is dragging too long—kids' lives at risk.)

Suddenly, a loud screaming voice came from behind us—across the road. I looked carefully—near a big tree on the opposite side, one old man in his 70s was scolding a group of 4-5 young college boys angrily, waving a stick. The boys were standing around a parked car, looking guilty. Curious—what happened? Police instinct kicked in. I decided to check, maybe I need help or something suspicious. I crossed the road carefully.

"What happened, Uncle Ji?" I asked politely.

"See these careless boys—almost killed me with their speeding car! Rash driving in narrow roads," he said angrily.

"No, sir—we didn't want to kill anyone. It was sudden," one boy said defensively.

"Now making excuses! Who gave you a driving license at this young age? Wait—I'll call the police right now," the old man threatened, taking out his phone.

"No, sir, please don't—we are sorry. We are going somewhere important, and suddenly a street dog came in front of the car. We applied hard brakes to save it—that's why the car swerved. So sorry if you got scared or hurt," the boy said very emotionally, almost pleading.

The old man calmed a bit.

"I hate this new generation—always speeding, phones in hand. Okay, but remember—never speed your car in such small residential roads again. Drive safe." He grumbled and left slowly. The boys sighed in relief.

"But where are you guys going in such a hurry?" I asked casually but curiously.

"Why should we tell you, uncle?" one bolder boy said rudely. "Because I am Inspector Veer—Mumbai Police," I replied calmly, showing ID quickly. All the boys went pale.

"Sorry, sir! We didn't know. But we are telling the truth about the dog."

"I believe that part. Now—what I asked you? Where were you rushing?" "We... we are going to a club—friend's birthday party, but he cancelled the plan", one said hesitantly.

"Why?"

"Our friend messaged the group just now—the plan was suddenly cancelled."

"So he tells you why it was cancelled?"

"He said the owner is not behaving normally today—acting scared. And some group of unknown men in suits came, some even carrying guns visible. Moving in and out of VIP rooms. He said it's not safe—better cancel." My mind alerted instantly.

"Tell me the club name—exactly."

"hm.....Name..."

"TELL ME FAST!" I said louder, urgently.

"C... Club... Club 21, sir!"

"Club 21—okay. You boys go home now—stay safe, no parties today." I rushed back across the road to our jeep. My brain started making many theories—gang meeting? Drug deal? Bablu involved?

"Dev! Let's go—we found something big," I shouted.

"What, sir?" Dev asked, running over.

"Club 21—something suspicious is happening there right now. Men with suits and guns, the owner scared, were emptying the club. I will explain everything in the car. Driver—fast to Club 21!" I told Dev the full story while calling other teams on the radio

"All teams converge at Club 21 immediately. Possible gang activity."

It took us 1 hour to reach—heavy evening traffic, signals, and narrow turns. All local teams were already there waiting outside—jeeps parked discreetly.

"You are talking about this club? Big one—Club 21?" Inspector Rawat confirmed.

"Yes. Let's go inside fast—quietly, no panic."

We entered the club entrance—big neon lights on now, music thumping lightly, but strangely, the whole club was almost empty. Only a few staff are cleaning. One waiter approached nervously.

"Sirs... club closed for private event today."

"Where is your manager?" I demanded.

"Upstairs VIP room, but..." We took out our guns carefully, safety on, and started moving upstairs silently—team formation. Reached a closed door.

I commanded one officer, "Check from the side window quietly." He peeked carefully.

"Only the manager inside the room, sir, alone, sitting tense."

"What! Only manager—no gang?" I said in confusion. Something wrong. I knocked on the door firmly. Manager opened—middle-aged, sweaty face.

"I knew this would happen... police coming," he said resignedly.

"What are you talking about? Where are the people with suits and guns? Why club empty?"

"What suits? What guns? What are you talking about?" The manager acted innocently.

"Stop this nonsense. We know everything. Why is this club completely empty in the evening?" Dev pressed. The manager sighed.

"Okay, I tell everything truthfully. I got an anonymous call around 6:45 PM—deep voice, threatening tone. Said 'Empty your club as much as possible by evening—send staff home early, cancel bookings. We need private use tonight.' Then transferred huge money online—lakhs of rupees. Said if I don't cooperate or inform the police, big trouble for my family."

"What? So you took money and emptied?"

"Yes... The amount was too much—I couldn't refuse. But I knew the police might come asking questions later. Now see—you guys are here."

"The whole thing was planned... fake diversion," I realised loudly.

"What, sir?" Dev asked.

"Whole thing—the old man fight, those boys' story about guns here—it was all set up! To mislead us, waste our time here."

"Why, sir?"

"Where were your teams at that time?" I asked Inspector Rawat.

"We were heading to our last club on the list—'neon'—big underground one."

"My theory: the real gang is at Neon Club right now—doing an important deal or meeting. When they got a tip somehow that your team was going there next, they quickly planned this fake story—paid boys or someone to create drama opposite road, spread rumour about guns here. So we all rush here—instead of neon. Gave them extra time to finish work and escape."

"Wow—what a clever plan. But why spend so much money and effort? Why not just run from neon when tip came?"

"I think the work they are doing tonight is very important—big drug deal or meeting very important person. Couldn't cancel or shift last minute. Needed that extra 1-2 hours desperately."

"Let's go to neon then—fast!" one constable said urgently.

"What do you think—they are still waiting for us there? It's almost 1.5 hours wasted already. They must have finished and vanished by now," Dev said realistically.

(Where is this case going—from a small missing teenager case to a big drug gang, diversions, all... What connection? Bablu must be key.)

CHAPTER TWELVE

NO WAY!

"It's almost time—clubs will close soon, people leaving. I think we should wrap everything up and try fresh tomorrow with a better plan," Inspector Rawat said, looking around the empty Club 21. He rubbed his tired eyes with a heavy sigh. The neon lights outside flickered, casting long shadows across the dance floor. The place felt hollow now, just empty chairs and the faint smell of stale smoke and perfume.

"Okay then, we will restart tomorrow morning," I agreed, though my mind was racing with new suspicions. Something felt off about how smoothly the night had been derailed. It was too neat, too convenient.

We started moving away from the club—teams packing up radios, voices tired, jeep engines coughing to life in the cool night.

"Our driver can drop you both wherever," Rawat offered again, patting my shoulder. His smile seemed friendly, but his eyes didn't quite meet mine.

"Thanks, sir, but no—we can manage by ourselves. Taxi or auto," I replied politely but firmly. I wanted to be alone with Dev, to talk freely.

"As you wish. But think overnight about next steps—we have to find that gang soon, and yes, your main suspect, Bablu. Keep me updated."

"Of course, sir. Good night."

He nodded and turned back to his men. Dev and I walked out into the street. After about 10 minutes of walking through the now quiet lanes—a cool wind blowing, shop shutters rattling down, stray dogs nosing through garbage—we spotted a taxi parked under a streetlight and hailed it.

The taxi was an old white Ambassador, its seats worn but clean. As we settled into the back, Dev spoke up, his voice low.

"What a mastermind plan, sir—a complete fake diversion with actors."

"The boy's emotional acting, the old man's anger—the timing was so perfect. How did I fall into their trap so easily? We wasted precious hours," I said, hitting my fist lightly on the seat. The frustration was a tight knot in my chest.

"The real question is—who is helping them from inside? Leaking our exact movements? Our driver today, any constable following, or even the Inspector himself?"

"I know, Dev. After today, we trust no one blindly."

The taxi moved through the sleeping city, past closed tea stalls and dimly lit apartment windows. The driver, a thin man with greying hair, had been silent, focusing on the road. But then he cleared his throat softly, as if gathering courage.

"I don't have the right to interfere in police matters, sir, but... can I tell you something I know?" he said carefully, his eyes glancing at us in the rearview mirror. They were earnest, worried.

"What is it? Speak freely," I said, leaning forward. "The whole local police station is involved in something wrong—a corrupt deal," he said, his voice steady but serious.

"What! How can you say that with such confidence?" Dev leaned forward, shocked.

"Sir, about a month ago, my close friend's bike was stolen from the market. We went together to file a complaint at the same station. While waiting in the queue, three rough-looking men were inside talking privately with the Inspector—the door was half closed. The constable told us to wait longer. Then two other constables standing nearby started gossiping in a low voice. One said worriedly, 'This is not good—we are police officers, how can we do this just for money? Betraying our duty.' The second one replied casually, 'Relax—it's a normal one-week deal only. We have to do just one simple thing: no surprise checking or raids in any clubs, understand? The boss gives double money this time—so what's the problem? Easy cash.' Sir, I heard it clearly. From that day, I never fully trusted any policeman here. Corruption is eating the system."

The weight of his words settled in the quiet cab. The only sound was the hum of the engine.

"Oh... that's a heavy allegation. Serious if true. But why should we believe you now? There's every chance you are also part of that gang—trying to misguide us, create doubt," I said, my voice hardening. After today's clever trick, paranoia was high. Everyone was a suspect.

The driver's hands tightened on the steering wheel. "Sir, I swear on my taxi—this vehicle is my only source of income, it feeds my family. It is like a god for a poor man like me. If you still don't believe after this swear, do whatever you want—arrest me, check my records, anything. But sir, we common people want a good, honest police system—one we can trust in trouble."

There was a raw honesty in his plea. Dev looked at me, his expression serious.

"Sir, I think he is speaking the truth. You saw how Inspector Rawat acted today—after we discovered no gang here, he was too quick to close the investigation for the day, no anger or urgency," Dev whispered.

I studied the driver's face in the mirror. His brow was furrowed, his lips pressed thin. He looked like a man carrying a burden.

"What is your name, bhai?" I asked, my tone softening.

"You can call me Ramu, sir—everyone does."

"Okay, Ramu—from now on, you will be our personal driver for this case. Pick up, drop, wherever wegoin Dehradun. Daily. But don't tell anyone about this conversation, about us, or about the case—not a word. But remember, strictly, if I find even a small hint that you are betraying us or are part of anything wrong, no one will be worse than me. Understand?"

"Okay, sir. Thank you for your trust. But one more time—I am not betraying you. I hate what's happening in this city—drugs everywhere because of such deals."

After 5 more minutes of driving—up the winding roads, past sleeping houses draped in darkness—we reached home. Warm yellow lights glowed from the windows, a welcoming feel against the cold night.

"Tomorrow sharp 8 AM—here at the gate," I told Ramu.

He nodded seriously, saved my number into an old basic phone, and drove off quietly into the night.

"Do you believe him fully, sir?" Dev asked as we walked to the door, our footsteps crunching on the gravel path.

"Eyes never lie, Dev. He was honest—the fear of a poor man, but the truth was shining through."

We entered the house quietly—trying not to disturb anyone. But suddenly all the lights in the hallway switched on brightly.

"Congratulations!" Mom and Dad said together excitedly, standing in the living room with plates full of sweets—ladoos, barfi, jalebi glistening with syrup.

Mohit was also there, leaning against the wall and grinning widely.

"What happened suddenly? Why congratulations?" I asked, confused but smiling at their happy faces.

"First eat this ladoo—sweet for good news. And you too, Dev beta," Mom said, feeding me one big ladoo forcefully, then popping one into Dev's mouth.

"Hmm... tasty as always. Now tell properly—what's the occasion?" I asked, the sweet dissolving on my tongue.

"Remember the girl you went to meet in the café back in Mumbai? Ruhi?"

"Yes, of course. So?"

"Her parents called today evening—full approval! She said YES properly. They liked you very much—your job, your family, everything."

"Oh... she said yes," I said, feeling a warm happiness spread through my chest. It was a bright, clean feeling after the grime of the day.

"Congratulations, sir! Great news," Dev said genuinely, patting my back.

"Thank you, Dev."

"Now you also say yes formally, and we start the wedding process—fix dates, roka ceremony, shopping, everything," Mom said, her eyes shining with excitement. She was already mentally planning.

"Yes, from my side also—fully, 100%," I confirmed, hugging Mom. She smelled of saffron and home.

"Perfect match! But be aware from now, beta—someone else is coming to rule the kingdom here," Dad joked, winking.

And we all started laughing loudly—a pure family joy after a tense, suspicious day. Then suddenly my phone rang—a saved number, Ruhi calling.

(Oh, it's her—perfect timing.)

"Excuse me one minute," I said and moved toward the terrace for privacy. The cool night breeze hit my face, a relief.

"So... you said yes?" I started with a teasing smile in my voice.

"Yes. I think you are the only one who properly understands me—my thoughts, my ambitions. You have a perfect job, perfect income, perfect health—my parents already love you like a son."

"And you personally?" I interrupted playfully.

"No!" she said seriously.

"What?.. So why did you..."

And she burst out laughing uncontrollably, a sound like bells.

"I am kidding, Veer! Of course, I like you a lot—that's why I said yes," she continued, laughter still in her words.

"You almost got me—my heart skipped a beat," I said with big relief, laughing too.

"So, tomorrow coffee to celebrate properly?"

"Actually... I am in Dehradun right now—for some urgent work case."

"Oh, so you are at your parents' home? A surprise visit?"

"Yes—the family is happy."

"I want to talk to your mom—properly, as a future daughter-in-law."

"Yes, why not. But don't be too familiar—don't gossip about my childhood secrets," I joked. And we both started laughing again, a warm, easy sound.

"Oh, Inspector sir—always duty first."

I started moving downstairs—Mom was in the kitchen now, teaching Dev a simple recipe, showing him how to make the perfect masala for mixed veg. The air was fragrant with ginger and cardamom.

"Wow, thank you, aunty—it's a perfect aroma already," Dev said, smelling the fresh ground spices.

"Mom, she wants to talk to you," I said, handing her the phone. Mom's face lit up like Diwali—she ran quickly, took the phone excitedly, and started walking around the living room talking.

"Hello, beta! How are you? Yes, we all are so happy here... tell me how your family is, how work is doing, everything..."

Along with mother-in-law, daughter-in-law chat began—Mom asking rapid-fire questions, laughing, her free hand gesturing wildly.

I signalled Dev with my eyes—come to the terrace quietly. He nodded, wiped his hands on a towel, and followed me back up the stairs.

The terrace was dark, lit only by the distant city glow and a slice of moon. It felt like a secret meeting place.

"We have very little time left now, Dev. The case is escalating—how do we find Bablu and the gang with possible corruption inside the local force?"

"I am still shocked about the police involvement—protecting drug deals for money."

"Money can buy everything, sadly, Dev—even uniforms. Now think fast—we need to search and find the Dehradun DSP sir's direct number or contact somehow. We have to inform him secretly about possible corruption in this station and request his direct help—maybe a special team."

"Yes, sir. And..."

We suddenly heard a low but clear "No!" voice from the nearby store room on the terrace. It was a boy's voice, but strained, tense.

"Who is that? Talking so late at night?"

I signalled Dev—keep quiet, finger on my lips. We moved silently down the stairs, our shadows long on the wall. The store room door was slightly ajar, a thin line of light spilling onto the floor of the dark corridor. Peeking carefully—my brother Mohit was inside, his back toward the door. He was on his phone, whispering tensely.

"No, bro... I cannot do this anymore. Please. My real brother is here now—he is a big police officer, IPS from Mumbai. Try to understand... It's too risky... someone will catch... okay, okay, I will try somehow... but no promises... bye."

He disconnected the call, looking scared and lost. He pocketed his phone and let out a shaky breath, his shoulders slumped.

As he turned around to come out, he saw us standing there, blocking the doorway.

His face went completely white—a mask of pure shock. The blood seemed to drain from his cheeks instantly.

"Tell us everything—right now. Who was that? What can you not do?" I said firmly, my voice low but serious. I stepped inside and closed the door behind us, shutting the three of us into the small, dusty room.

The air felt still and heavy. Boxes were piled around us. Mohit's eyes darted from my face to Dev's and back, like a trapped animal.

"Bhaiya, I..." he stammered, his voice barely a whisper.

"Start talking, Mohit. No lies," I said, my heart pounding with a dreadful mix of professional duty and personal fear. My own brother. What had he gotten himself into?

He swallowed hard, his Adam's apple bobbing. The single bulb above us flickered, casting jumping shadows across his terrified face.

CHAPTER THIRTEEN

Birthday Party

'Sorry, Bhaiya... It's not my fault,' he stammered, his voice cracking. He looked down at his shoes, unable to meet my gaze.

'First, tell me who you were talking with?' I said, keeping my voice steady. The small storeroom felt even smaller, the air thick with dust and tension.

'Karan... he's a friend of mine,' Mohit whispered.

'What are you talking about with him? What can't you do anymore?'

He shuffled his feet. 'Something has been wrong in our school for months.'

'What kind of wrong?'

'Students... they are buying stuff and...'

'What kind of stuff, Mohit?'

He finally looked up, his eyes wide with a fear I'd never seen in my little brother before. 'It's like a white powder. In small packets.'

A cold dread settled in my stomach. 'Have you tried any?' I asked, my voice dropping to a serious, low tone.

'No! I swear, never. I promise on Mom and Dad,' he said, the words rushing out. 'I know what it is. I know what it does.'

'So who is this Karan, and what are you talking about with him?'

'He's... like a broker for these things. Students give money to him, and the next day he gives them the stuff. But he's a very good friend of mine. I always tell him to leave all this and do something for your career, but he never listens to me.' Mohit's shoulders slumped.

'Tomorrow is his birthday, and he is inviting me to a club to celebrate, but... I don't know why, I have a bad feeling about this club.'

'Why? What's special about this club?'

'This club is very secret. You cannot find its name on any map. It's like an old building with no boards or signs. But if you enter from the back side, you get entry into the club. A place where you can get... everything you want.' His voice was barely a whisper now.

Dev and I exchanged a sharp look. This sounded exactly like the kind of shadowy operation Bablu would use.

'We need your help,' I said, making a split-second decision.

'What kind of help?' Mohit asked, confused and scared.

'When does your friend's birthday party begin?'

'He said 6 PM to me. But why?'

'Okay. You are going with him, but with a little change in the plan.' I paused, making sure he was listening. 'You will wear a hidden Bluetooth mic and earpiece so we can hear everything and communicate with you. Okay?'

'But, Bhaiya...' he started, panic rising in his eyes.

'You need to ask him about Bablu. Tell him you want to meet him.'

'Who is this Bablu? And what if he asks why?'

'He is the one we are here for. And Karan is your friend—you know how to get words out of him,' Dev said, stepping closer.

'Get it?' I pressed.

'Yes...' Mohit said slowly. 'But promise me you'll do nothing to Karan. Please. He's... he's just confused.'

'We'll see. Go now, it's late already,' I said, opening the storeroom door. The normal sounds of the house felt alien.

'Okay, Bhaiya. Good night.'

'Good night.'

As Mohit hurried to his room, Dev let out a slow breath. "Ghar mein chhora, sheher mein dindora," he said softly—a boy at home, a drumbeat announcing trouble in the city. And we both laughed a short, tense laugh. The irony was heavy.

'Let's go to sleep, it's really late,' I said, and we moved downstairs. My mind was already racing ahead, planning for tomorrow.

' I am sooooo tired,' Dev groaned, stretching his arms.

'Going to sleep without eating?' Mom's voice came from the kitchen doorway. She stood there with her hands on her hips, a look of motherly disapproval on her face.

'Oh, we haven't eaten anything since morning because of this case. We weren't even feeling hungry,' I said, realising my own stomach was empty.

'Now I am starting to feel hungry,' Dev admitted.

We all laughed, the sound easing the tightness in the room. Mom quickly warmed up the leftover dal and rotis, and sabji. We ate in comfortable silence at the kitchen table, the food simple and grounding.

After eating, we went to our room. Just as I was about to lie down, my phone rang. I checked—it was Anil from Mumbai.

'Hello, Anil. How are you?' ' I'm fine, sir. Any update?' His voice was tense.

'Yes, we have a lead. A strong one.'

'Oh, that's really good. Actually, sir...' He hesitated.

'What is it?'

' In school, everyone is saying that the police are doing nothing. They are thinking of talking to the media, so it will become big news. They think it will be easier to find the dealers if there's pressure.'

'What! No, Anil, stop them from doing that. It will create a mess! It will alert the gang.'

' I am trying, sir. But there is a group of boys who are not listening. They are saying that if there is no update in the next two days, they will tell everything to the media. One of the boy's fathers is the head of "MK News," and you know that's the number one news channel in Mumbai.' Anil's voice was full of worry.

'Yes, I know,' I said, my heart sinking. I knew the channel head well—a man who loved sensational stories and had a deep distrust of the police. 'We are trying our best. Tell them that. Plead with them.'

'Okay, sir. I have to go now, my mom is calling. Good night.'

'Good night, Anil.' I ended the call and threw my phone on the bed.

'SHIT!'

'What happened, sir?' Dev asked, already sitting up.

The school boys are thinking of telling everything to MK News in two days if we don't show progress.'

'What! MK News? Sir, their head doesn't like police work. He always speaks against us.'

'I know, Dev. If this hits the news, Bablu will see it and run. We have to catch him within two days, or he'll vanish. My brother's friend is our last hope now.' The weight of the deadline pressed down on me. 'Let's go to sleep, Dev. We need clear heads.'

'Yes, sir.'

Next Day (7th Day of Missing)

'Wake up, Dev. Lots of work today,' I said, shaking him gently.

The morning light was pale through the curtains.

'Yes, sir,' he mumbled, rubbing his eyes.

We refreshed up and moved to the dining table for breakfast. The smell of ghee and fresh parathas filled the air and Uttrakhand special sabji (lingud ki sabji), also known as Fiddlehead Ferns. It is a highly sought-after wild vegetable that grows naturally in moist areas, And so good for health.

'One more, Dev beta?' my mom asked, beaming, as we had already eaten three each.

'No, Aunty, I am full. These taste so delicious,' Dev said, patting his stomach.

'Thank you, Dev. But you have to eat one more. For strength,' Mom insisted, holding the plate.

'No, Aunty, please! What if we have to run today? Sir is fit, he can easily. I am the one who is going to struggle,' Dev said, making a dramatic face.

My mom laughed, finally relenting. 'Okay, okay. But drink your milk.'

'Let's go, Mohit!' I called out as he was coming out of his room, dressed casually in jeans and a hoodie

. 'Yes, Bhaiya, just two minutes!' he replied, scrambling for his bag.

'Where is Mohit going? Don't put him in any danger,' Mom said, her smile fading into concern.

'No, Mom, I am just dropping him at his friend's house. Today is his friend's birthday,' I said, giving her a reassuring smile.

'But...' she began. The taxi horn sounded outside, interrupting her.

'Okay, Mom, we have to go. Mohit! Fast!' We exited our home and saw Ramu waving from his taxi. He gave a small, serious nod. We got in.

'Now tell me, sir, where do we go?' Ramu asked, pulling onto the quiet morning street.

'Do you know any man who can provide us with Bluetooth speakers and a mic? Small, hidden ones?' Dev asked.

Ramuthought for a moment, his eyes on the road. Hmm... yes. I know one man who has these kinds of gadgets. He has an electronics store, but he is a bit... different.'

'Let's go, then,' I said. As we moved, my phone rang. I checked—it was Inspector Rawat.

'Hello, sir. Where are you?' His voice was casual, but there was an edge to it.

' I'm fine, Inspector. Actually, I am going back to Mumbai for some urgent work,' I lied smoothly. 'Oh? So when will you come back?'

' It will take some time. You keep the investigation going. If you find something solid, then call me.'

'Okay, sir,' he said, and the call ended. His tone had been a little too easy, a little too accepting.

'How long will it take to reach this man?' Dev asked Ramu.

'About one hour, sir. He lives on the outskirts.'

We finally reached a quieter, older part of the city. The houses were bigger, set back behind walls. Ramu stopped in front of a black iron gate. The house behind it was painted a deep blue. 'This one, sir. The black gate house.' Werang the bell. A young boy, maybe sixteen, opened the door. He looked us up and down.

'Yes?'

'We are here to meet Guru Ji,' Ramu said respectfully.

'Come in.' We entered. The house was unlike any electronics store owner's home I'd seen.

The walls were covered with pictures and statues of gods—Krishna, Shiva, Ganesha. The air smelled of incense and sandalwood. We sat on a large, worn sofa. After five minutes, a man around forty entered. He was wearing a simple white dhoti and kurta, but a heavy gold watch gleamed on his wrist. He had one diamond earring and a full, well-trimmed beard. His presence was calm but sharp.

'Namaskar, Bhaiya,' Ramu said, folding his hands.

'Hare Krishna,' the man replied, his voice deep and serene.

'Now, tell me, what brings you here?'

'Bhaiya, these are my friends. They need something from your store, but my friend told me you closed your store five days ago. That's why we came here.'

'Oh,' the man said, a small smile on his lips. 'Actually, my daughter is getting married. I am not getting time to open it.' He looked at me, his gaze piercing.

'Congratulations, sir,' I said. He nodded in acknowledgement.

'You can do one thing. Go with my man to the store, and he will give you what you want.'

'Okay, sir. Thank you for your help.'

' It is my duty to help,' he said simply. He then called out, and a lean, efficient-looking worker appeared from another room. We said our goodbyes and exited the spiritually charged atmosphere of the house. Outside, the worker said,

'Sir knows Ramu well. Otherwise, he would never open the store for one person.'

'How long will it take?' Dev asked.

'Not much. Only ten minutes. Follow me.'

He got on his bike and gestured for us to follow in the taxi. After a ten-minute drive through winding lanes, we reached a shuttered shop in a market that was just beginning to wake up.

The sign above it read 'Guru Electronics' in faded letters. The worker took out a large set of keys, unlocked the heavy shutter, and rolled it up with a loud clatter. Inside, the store was a treasure trove. Shelves were packed with all kinds of gadgets— drones, cameras, headphones, and boxes of imported electronics. There were also stacks of unusual clothing, like jackets with many pockets and hats with strange bulges.

'Now, tell me, what do you want?'

'We need a Bluetooth microphone, a button-like camera and a tiny earpiece, so we can communicate from a long distance without being seen,' Ramu explained.

'Okay. Give me a minute.'

The worker moved towards a locked glass cabinet at the back. While he was gone, I let my eyes wander. Among the usual electronics, one small device on a high shelf caught my eye. It was black, no bigger than a coin, with a tiny, steady red light. It looked professional. After a minute, the worker returned with a small, sleek box.

'Here it is, sir. Latest version. Very good range, very clear.'

'How much?' Dev asked.

'Ten thousand. But Sir said to give an extra discount for his daughter's wedding, so you have to pay only seven thousand.'

'Oh, that's great,' Dev said.

'What is that?' I asked, pointing to the small device with the red light.

'That's a GPS tracker, sir. But you cannot buy it,' he replied, his tone turning cautious.

'Why?'

'You have to take special permission from the police and submit the paperwork to us. Only then can we give you that tracker. It is not a normal one you can buy online. It is used by police and government agents. Very powerful, very accurate.' He folded his arms.

'We are police,' Dev said, reaching for his wallet. The man's eyes widened.

'What? How can I believe you?'

Dev took out his official ID card and showed it. The man peered at it closely, his demeanour changing instantly.

'Oh! Sorry, sir. Of course, you can have it. Here, write your name and details in this register, and then I will give it to you.' He fetched a thick, leather-bound ledger.

'How much for the tracker?'

'Sir told me that if any policeman comes to buy that tracker, give a 40% discount. So, with the mic and earpiece, your total is twenty thousand.'

I handed him my card and filled out the register carefully, noting down my badge number and the case reference.

'Thank you, sir,' he said, wrapping the devices carefully in newspaper.

'Be careful. This tracker is very strong. It can even work through two floors of concrete.' We left the store, the morning sun now bright and warm. Mohit, who had been quiet the whole time, finally spoke up.

'Now what?' he asked, looking at the packages in my hands.

'First, we will check that all these things are working properly,' I replied.

'Where will we put this camera?' Dev asked, holding up the tiny lens that came with the mic.

'On his shirt, replacing a button?' Mohit suggested.

'No. Anyone who looks closely might see that one button is different,' I said.

'So where, then?' Dev asked. I looked at Mohit's shirt.

'On his wrist. The button of his shirt cuff. It won't come into direct eye contact, and no one will notice a shirt button there. We'll replace the tiny camera lens with the button that looks normal.'

'Oh, that's smart,' Mohit said, a flicker of admiration in his scared eyes.

'We need to move to a hotel where we can fix this properly,' I said to Ramu.

'Okay, sir. I have a cousin who manages the "Vasanta Hotel." It's quiet. And... I have a small sewing kit in the taxi. My wife keeps it for emergencies. We can fix the shirt there.'

We started moving. It took about an hour to reach the Vasanta Hotel, a modest, clean building on a quieter street.

' I have some other work to do nearby, sir. Call me on the other number whenever you are ready,' Ramu said, dropping us off.

I noted his number again, and we entered the hotel. We checked into a room on the second floor—simple, with two beds and a table. As soon as we entered, Dev's phone rang.

'Excuse me, sir, my mom is calling,' he said and stepped out into the hallway for privacy.

I asked Mohit for the formal shirt he had brought for the party—a crisp blue one—and laid it on the table. I took out the tiny camera lens, the modified button, and the small sewing kit. Mohit sat on the edge of the bed, watching.

'Sorry, Bhaiya,' he said suddenly, his voice soft.

'Why?' I asked, not looking up from my work.

'For having friends like these. For getting mixed up in this. I promise, I never took any pill or powder.'

I stopped and looked at him. His eyes were sincere, filled with the regret of a younger brother who'd disappointed his idol.

'Hmm... I believe you.' 'Thank you, Bhaiya,' he said, relief washing over his face.

'And... tell me anything else. How is your school going? How is your life?' I began carefully stitching the button. 'Actually, I am also sorry because I don't give you time to ask you these things.'

' It's okay, Bhaiya. I know how important this case is for you. And about my life... yes, it's good. We won the city football cup last month.'

'Oh, yes! Mom was telling me about that. Show me a photo.'

He took out his phone from his pocket, his face lighting up a little. He swiped through it and then handed it to me. The photo showed him, muddy and beaming, holding a trophy. His teammates were cheering around him.

'Wow, Mohit. Good!' I said, zooming in.

'Who is this girl on your side? She looks more excited than you!'

'No one! Just a friend,' he said quickly, snatching the phone back, a faint blush on his cheeks.

'Hmm...friend or something else?' I said, giving him a knowing smile as I went back to stitching.

'No, Bhaiya, just friends.'

'Show me your chats, then?' I teased.

'What! Chats? Bhaiya!' he exclaimed, horrified, and I couldn't help but laugh.

'Just kidding. What's her name, by the way?'

'Palak,' he mumbled, blushing harder.

'And how long has this relatio.... I mean, friendship has been going on?'

'One year, five months, two weeks, and... five days,' he said, counting in his head.

I watched him. He was trying to hide a smile, looking at the floor.

(This is a whole teenage problem, why count every day?)

'And your studies?' I asked, changing the subject.

He covered his face with his hands and groaned.

'I am working on it...' he said in a low, sheepish voice. Just then, Dev entered the room.

'All good. Mom just wanted to say hello.' He saw the shirt. 'Done?'

'Almost. Here, wear this,' I said, handing the shirt to Mohit.

He put it on. It looked perfect—a normal, smart shirt for a party.

'Which hand did you place the camera on?' Dev asked, peering at the cuffs.

'That's what I want, no one can notice,' I said. I took out my phone and opened the companion app for the device. I paired it with the camera. After a moment, the screen lit up.

'Yes... perfect! I can see everything.' The view was from Mohit's wrist, showing the hotel room from a low angle.

'Rotate your hand slowly... yes, perfect. The image is stable and clear.'

'Now it's time for the Bluetooth earbuds,' Dev said, opening the other box. I read the instructions and then carefully placed the tiny, flesh-colored earbud in Mohit's ear. It was virtually invisible.

'Where is your winter cap? The black one you always wear?' I asked. He pulled it from his bag. It was a simple beanie. He put it on, pulling it down just over his ears.

'Perfect, sir. No one will doubt it. It just looks like he's feeling cold,' Dev said, inspecting him from all sides.

Mohit stood in the middle of the room, looking like any other teen going to a party, but now he was our eyes and ears.

'Now we have to just wait for the phone call from Karan,' I said, looking into both their eyes. The room was quiet. The calm before the storm. Mohit's birthday party began at 6 PM. We had eight hours to prepare, to plan, and to hope that a scared teenager could help us trap a dangerous drug lord.

CHAPTER FOURTEEN

The Delivery

The clock on the wall ticked slowly. It was 6 PM. The party was supposed to start now. But Mohit's phone was quiet.

Dev sat on the couch, then stood up and walked around. He sat down again. Mohit watched a movie on TV, but he was not really watching. I lay on the bed, looking at the ceiling. We were all waiting. The room was very quiet. It felt heavy.

"Maybe he changed his mind. Maybe he knows something," Dev said.

"He will call. He is Mohit's friend," I said. I wanted to believe it.

At 6:30, nothing. Mohit checked his phone again and again.

Then, at 6:45, a loud ringtone broke the silence. We all jumped.

"Who is it?" I asked, sitting up.

Mohit looked at the screen. "It's Mom."

He answered. "Yes, Mom? I am at my friend's house... I have to go to his birthday party soon... Yes, I will be back before 9... Okay, bye."

He put the phone down. "No news."

"When will your friend call?" Dev asked, his voice tight.

"I don't know. He said 6," Mohit said, worried.

"What about the guard at the gate? How will you get past?" I asked.

"Everyone knows Karan there. The guard never checks me. He just waves me in," Mohit replied.

"Good. One problem less," Dev said.

7:00 PM. Still no call. The sun was going down outside. The room was getting dark.

"I don't think he—" Dev started to say.

Then Mohit's phone buzzed loudly. The screen lit up with the name: KARAN. Mohit and I stood up fast. Dev was next to us in a second.

"Answer. Be normal. Be happy," I told him quietly.

Mohit took a deep breath and answered. "Hello, Karan! Where are you? I have been waiting!" He listened. "Yes... The party started already?... Okay, I will come now... Who?... Okay, bye."

He put the phone down. His eyes were big. "He said the party started an hour ago. He was busy. He told me to come now. And... he said he wants me to meet someone special."

"Who?" Dev asked quickly.

"He did not say. He just said, 'You will see.' We have to go now."

"Yes. Dev, call Ramu. We have to leave right now," I said, grabbing my jacket and the small screen for the camera.

"Calling," Dev said.

We rushed out of the hotel room. The evening air was cool. Ten minutes later, Ramu's white taxi came around the corner. He saw us and stopped.

"Where is the club?" Ramu asked as we got in. I sat in front. Dev and Mohit got in the back.

"It has no name. I will tell you the way," Mohit said, leaning forward.

Mohit told Ramu where to go. "Turn left here." "Right at the tea shop." "Go straight down this small road." We drove into an old part of the city. The nice shops were gone. Now the buildings were old and the paint was peeling. After thirty minutes, we came to a street with closed warehouses.

"There," Mohit whispered, pointing. "That low building. The one with no paint."

It was a two-floor concrete building. It looked empty. The front was shut with a rusty metal door. No sign, no lights. We stopped the taxi about six shops away, under a big tree.

I turned to look at Mohit. His face was pale. "All set? Earbud in? Camera button on?" I asked.

He nodded. He fixed his winter cap. The tiny camera was hidden on his shirt cuff. The earbud was hidden under his cap.

"Good. Now go. Be natural. Be his friend. We can hear you. We can see you. You are not alone."

He nodded stiffly. He opened the door and got out. He took a deep breath, put his hands in his pockets, and walked toward the back of the building. My heart beat hard.

As soon as he was far enough, I opened the app on my phone. The screen lit up. It showed a shaky view of the ground as Mohit walked. We could hear his breathing through the audio.

"We can see and hear. Good," Dev said, looking over my shoulder.

On the screen, we saw Mohit go to the back of the building. There was a heavy metal door. Two big men in dark jackets stood there. They were bodyguards. They crossed their arms as Mohit came close.

Mohit stopped and called on his phone. We heard the ring through our feed. "Karan, I am at the back door." He waited. "Okay."

We waited. Three long minutes passed. Then the metal door opened. Loud music and colored light spilled out. A boy stepped into view.

"Hey, brother! You came!" It was Karan. He was tall and thin with styled hair and a shiny silver chain. He hugged Mohit.

"Happy birthday, Karan," Mohit said. He sounded cheerful.

"Come inside! Many fun things are waiting!" Karan laughed. He put an arm around Mohit's shoulders and led him inside. The door closed behind them with a heavy sound.

For a moment, the screen went dark. Then the camera adjusted. My breath caught. Dev made a low sound next to me.

The camera showed a big, dim hall. Flashing lights came from a DJ booth. The air was full of smoke. The room was full of young people—boys and girls from maybe sixteen to twenty-two years old. They were drinking from bottles and glasses. They were smoking. It was wrong to see such young faces doing these things.

"Oh God," Dev whispered from the side seat. He had looked at the screen. "They are just children."

"Everyone, Mohit is here!" Karan said to a group nearby. Some people lifted their bottles to say hello. Mohit's camera shook as he shook hands.

"How are you, Captain?" one boy asked, his words slurred.

"I am fine. How are you?" Mohit replied.

"Want a drink?" another friend asked, holding out a bottle.

"NO!" I said firmly into the mic connected to Mohit's earpiece.

On screen, Mohit gently pushed the bottle away. "No, I am fine. Thanks."

He turned back to Karan. "You said you had to introduce me to someone?"

"Oh, yes! Come, my special friends want to meet you. They are in the back room." Karan led him away from the main hall, down a short hallway. They stopped at a door painted bright red. Karan knocked twice and opened it.

The view changed as they went in. This room was smaller and quieter. A red lamp gave the only light. Five men sat on big leather sofas. They were older, maybe late twenties or thirties. They wore nice clothes—silk shirts, good jeans. Each had a wine glass. They stopped talking and looked up.

Dev's eyes went wide. "There..." he breathed.

"Here, sir. My friend, Mohit," Karan said. He sounded very respectful now.

One of the men, a big man with a gold chain, leaned forward. "Hello, Mohit. Karan has told me about you." His voice was smooth.

"Hello, sir. Nice to meet you," Mohit said. The camera showed the man's face clearly.

"Come, have a drink. Have fun. It is your best friend's birthday."

"No, sir I don't drink. You all enjoy."

Another man, thin with sharp eyes, pointed at Mohit's head. "Why are you wearing that winter cap? It looks bad."

Before Mohit could answer, the first man hit the thin man's arm playfully. "Don't listen to him. Wear what you like."

"Ask their names," I told Mohit quietly.

"What are your names, sir?" Mohit asked politely.

"Why?" the thin man said, his face suddenly serious. Then he laughed, and the others laughed too. "Just joking, boy! I am Ganesh. He is Uday, that is Dheraj, Daya, and that one sitting far in the corner, we call him Black Monkey!" He laughed loudly.

The man in the corner looked up. He did not smile. "Don't listen to them, Mohit. They are fools." His voice was calm and low. It had authority. "My name is BABLU."

My heart beat fast. Bablu. On the screen, the camera held on his face. It was him. Exactly like the police drawing—the sharp jaw, the cool eyes. He wore a blue jacket and black pants.

"Finally," Dev whispered. "That is the one."

"Go closer to him. Get a better look, but be casual," I told Mohit.

"Nice to meet you, sir," Mohit said, taking a few steps into the room. The camera showed Bablu clearly now.

"I am the richest one here," Bablu said with a slow, proud smile.

"You have an Audi. That does not make you the richest," Ganesh said, nudging him.

An Audi. I remembered something. I closed my eyes. I saw our drive to this street. "Yes! A black Audi! When we turned onto this road, there was a black Audi parked on the left side, under the broken streetlight!" I said to Dev.

"Ramu, take the taxi back toward that turn. Go slow," Dev said.

"Yes, sir," Ramu said. He put the car in reverse and rolled back quietly.

On screen, Mohit was talking. "I like Audis."

"You want a ride? We can go after the party," Bablu said, looking amused.

"Actually—" Mohit started to say.

Bablu's phone buzzed loudly on the table. He picked it up. His face changed from relaxed to serious. He listened and said, "Yes." He stood up.

"Guys, we have to go."

"Why? The party is fun!" Uday said.

"Delivery," Bablu said simply. The other men put down their glasses and stood up fast.

"What about my birthday? At least wait for the cake cutting!" Karan said, looking sad.

Bablu looked at him. "Okay. Be fast. We have no time."

They all went back to the main hall. A birthday cake with sparkly candles was brought out. Karan cut it and gave pieces to Bablu and his men. They took them, but looked impatient.

"Dev, hurry! They are coming out!" I said, watching the screen.

Outside, where Ramu had moved us, we could see the black Audi under the faint light. Dev was already out of the taxi. He had the small tracker in his hand. He ran across the street, staying in the shadows.

"I am making the grip of the magnet very strong. Otherwise, it might fall on bad roads," Dev's voice came through my phone.

"They are saying goodbye. They are at the door!" I told him.

On the feed, Bablu patted Karan's shoulder. "Okay, Karan, happy. Now we go."

They walked out of the building. Just then, Dev slid out from under the Audi and ran back to us. He hid behind some old boxes as the back door opened.

Two minutes later, the five men came out into the night. They talked quietly, then all got into the Audi. The engine started, and the car drove away down the street.

"Mohit," I spoke into the mic. "I am sending you money for a taxi. Go straight home. Do not eat or drink anything. We have to follow them."

"Okay," Mohit's quiet voice came back. He sounded relieved.

"Ramu, let's go. We have the tracker. Take a different way out so they don't see a car following," Dev said, getting back into the taxi.

I turned on the tracker's screen. A small green dot blinked on the map. It was moving. "Got them. They are going north, to the old highway."

We drove off, keeping far back, watching the tracker. For almost an hour, the green dot moved on the highway, away from the city lights. It got darker outside.

"They are just driving. Do you know where they might go?" Dev asked Ramu.

"Not sure, sir. This highway goes to the old work area and... the unfinished places."

"They are turning left," I said, watching the dot leave the main road.

"Left?" Ramu looked surprised. "If they go left, the only thing there is the new train station. The one they stopped building months ago. It is empty."

"Yes," I remembered. "I read about that. People protested, and they stopped the work."

"That is why they go there. It is a good place for illegal work—far away, empty, no people. But it is very quiet. We must be very careful," Dev said. His hand touched his gun.

The green dot slowed and stopped. "They stopped," I said.

We drove slowly down the small road to the building site. In the distance, we saw the shape of the unfinished train station against the night sky—just concrete pillars and steel rods, with a fence around it. We stopped our taxi far away, hidden behind a pile of dirt.

On the tracker, the dot was not moving. With binoculars, we saw the Audi parked near a small site office. One man—it looked like Uday—got out. He went into the office and came out with a big black bag. He put it in the Audi's trunk and got back in. The car started moving again.

"They took the delivery. Now they will sell it," Ramu said.

I looked at Dev and smiled a little. He smiled back

(I think someone is more serious than us). We were close now.

We followed the blinking dot for another thirty minutes. It went back toward the edge of the city. It stopped in an area that looked like a shopping place.

"Where did they stop?" Dev asked, looking at the map.

"I think... it is the parking lot of that big mall. The one on the east side."

We drove there, taking a long way around. The mall was open. The parking lot was huge and almost full.

"Ramu, wait here near the back door. When Dev gives a missed call, that is the signal. Block the main exit with your taxi. We will catch them there. Dev, have your handcuffs ready. We must hold Bablu tight."

They both nodded, their faces serious. Dev and I got out of the taxi and walked into the shadows of the parking lot pillars. The air was cold and smelled of oil.

Using the tracker, we found the Audi in the underground parking. We took the stairs down, walking quietly. The underground level had bad lights—some spots were bright, some were dark. Our footsteps echoed a little.

Suddenly, Dev held up his fist. I stopped. He pointed between two parked vans. I moved next to him.

There was the black Audi. And there was Bablu. He leaned against the car door, a cigarette in his mouth. The black bag was near his feet. He was alone, looking at his phone. He was waiting.

"He is waiting for someone. A buyer," Dev whispered.

Five minutes passed. Then, from the other end, a person walked over. It was a young man, maybe nineteen. He wore a face mask, a low baseball cap, and a long black coat. He walked up to Bablu. They talked, but we were too far to hear.

"I will go closer. I need to hear," I whispered to Dev.

"There is a delivery van near them. You can hide behind it," Dev said, pointing.

I nodded. I signaled that I was going. I moved from pillar to pillar, using cars as cover. I reached the big white van and pressed against its cold side. Now I was close. I could hear them.

"Payment?" Bablu asked. He sounded bored.

"I have a card," the boy said. His voice shook.

"Give me the card machine," Bablu said. He turned and reached into the car window. He pulled out a small machine.

The boy took out a debit card and gave it to him.

"How much do you want?" a voice asked from inside the car. It was Ganesh.

"One pack," the boy said.

Bablu laughed a short laugh. "You don't have enough money for one pack, boy."

"What? I have twelve thousand in my bank!"

"One pack is fifteen thousand now," Ganesh's voice said from the car.

"What! But my friend told me it is twelve!"

"Yes, it was twelve. But a stupid police inspector is looking for us, so it is risky now. Fifteen."

The boy's voice broke. "Please, Bhaiya, I beg you. I can't... I can't sleep without it. Please."

"What to do?" Bablu said, looking at the car.

"Give him the paper," Ganesh's voice said.

Bablu took out a small notepad and a pen. "Sign this paper. It says you will pay the other three thousand at this address in one week. If you don't, we know where you live. Or... go away."

"Okay, okay, I will pay. Just give me the pack."

Bablu took a small plastic packet from the black bag. He swiped the boy's card and gave it back with a paper. Then he gave the boy the packet. The boy held it tight and ran away into the dark.

I signaled to Dev with my hand: Get ready.

Bablu watched the boy leave. He threw his cigarette on the ground. He said something to the men in the car and pointed to the far wall.

"Where are you going?" Ganesh's voice called.

Bablu waved his hand. "Need to use the toilet."

This is the moment.

I signaled Dev to stay and wait. As Bablu turned and walked toward the restroom sign, I followed him quietly, keeping cars between us. He pushed open the heavy restroom door, and I went in a few seconds after him.

The bathroom had bright, flickering lights. It smelled clean. Bablu stood at a urinal, his back to me. I walked to the sink next to him and turned on the water, pretending to wash my hands.

He finished and came to the sink beside me. He took out a cigarette and put it in his mouth. He patted his pockets.

He looked at me.

"Do you have a lighter?" he asked, the cigarette moving with his words.

I looked at him. I let a slow, cold smile come to my face. "No," I said.

"Shit, man," he said, turning to leave.

"But I think Shiva has a lighter," I added. My voice was flat and hard.

He froze. He turned his head slowly to look at me. His eyes were confused, then scared. "Wh... who... who are you?" he stammered.

I took out my police ID. I held it up so the badge shone in the light. "You are under arrest, Bablu. For taking Ajay and Sital. And for much more."

His eyes got very wide. For a second, he did not move. Then fear took over. He dropped his cigarette and ran for the door. He pushed it open hard and right into Dev. Dev stood straight in his path. He held his police gun with both hands, aimed right at Bablu's chest.

"Don't try to run, baby," Dev said. His voice was like ice.

Bablu stopped fast. His hands went up. His face was full of shock and anger.

CHAPTER FIFTEEN

FUN ZONE

'I have done nothing!' Bablu shouted. His eyes were wide, trying to look innocent.

'We will decide that later,' I said, keeping my voice steady. 'First, you message your friends. Tell them you have some other work and you have to go somewhere else. And if you try to be clever, we will take action. You saw Dev has a gun.'

Dev stepped forward and showed him the gun, making sure Bablu saw it clearly. Bablu's tough act faded. He looked at the gun and then at our faces. He was scared now.

He gave a small nod and took out his phone from his jacket pocket. He started typing a message with his thumbs. I moved right next to him so I could see the screen.

'Hey Ganesh, I have some work, so I am leaving. You guys go ahead without me,' Bablu typed.

A reply came almost instantly. 'Where? And what about your car?'

'I told you about that girl. She is calling me right now,' Bablu texted back, a weak excuse.

'Oh, have fun then. I will park your car at the office. But don't be late. We have the RED MEETING tonight,' came the reply.

'Ok, I will be there,' Bablu typed and hit send. The moment he did, I snatched the phone from his hand.

'Now tell me, what do you guys really want from me?' he said, trying to sound bold again, but his voice shook a little.

Just then, Dev's phone rang, breaking the tense silence. He answered quickly, his eyes on Bablu. 'Yes, Ramu?... Don't do anything. Just let them go.' He hung up and gave me a sharp nod. I understood. Ramu had seen the other men leave and wanted to know what to do.

'I said something! Are you guys deaf?' Bablu yelled, trying to take control of the situation.

Without a word, I stepped forward and slapped him hard across the face. The sound was sharp and loud in the quiet, concrete space of the parking garage.

'Not another word from you,' I said. My voice was low and left no room for argument.

I motioned to Dev with my eyes. He understood and reached for the handcuffs on his belt. As Dev looked down for just one second to unclip them, Bablu saw his chance. With a sudden burst of energy, he shoved Dev hard with both hands. Dev stumbled back, hitting the side of a parked car. Bablu spin around and sprinted into the dark maze of pillars.

'SHIT! Dev, run!' I yelled.

We both took off after him. Bablu was fast and knew the garage. He weaved between cars and dashed for the stairwell door. He yanked it open and disappeared upstairs, heading toward the mall's main level. We followed, our footsteps echoing loudly as we charged up the concrete steps.

We burst out onto the crowded ground floor of the mall. Bright lights, music, and the noise of hundreds of people hit us. Shoppers carrying bags, families with strollers, groups of teenagers—it was a sea of movement. For a second, I lost him. Then I saw a flash of a blue jacket as Bablu shoved past a family, running straight for the bright, noisy entrance to the indoor fun zone.

'He's going into the games area!' I shouted to Dev over the mall noise.

We ran after him, pushing through the crowd as politely but firmly as we could.

(I can't take out my gun here. There are too many women and children. Too much risk.)

We entered the fun zone. The atmosphere changed instantly. The ceiling was lower, the lights were flashy and dim, and loud arcade music and sound effects blared from every direction. It was a jungle of blinking lights and laughing kids. Dev caught up to me, breathing hard.

'I told Ramu to block the mall's main exit with the taxi. He can't get out of the building,' Dev said, wiping his forehead.

'I lost sight of him. He's in here somewhere, but there are so many people, and it's so dark...' I said, feeling a knot of panic in my stomach. We could not lose him now, not after getting so close.

'I'll go search the left side, through the ticket games and the bumper cars,' Dev said, and he moved off quickly.

I stood still for a moment, turning in a slow circle. My eyes scanned the shadows and the glowing game screens. Then I saw a tall, bored-looking man leaning against a pillar near a row of racing games. He was just watching the crowd, looking like he was waiting for someone.

I walked over to him. 'Hey, I need your help,' I said, keeping my voice urgent but calm.

'Yes? How can I help you?' he asked, looking a bit surprised.

'I need you to stand right at the exit of this fun zone,' I said, pointing to the archway that led back to the mall. 'Don't let any man in a blue jacket and black pants leave. He's about this tall,' I said, holding my hand up to Bablu's height.

The man stared at me, then started to laugh. It was a dry, disbelieving laugh. 'Why would I do that? Look, I'm just bored because my kids are in there playing games and I have to wait for them. That doesn't mean I'm going to do a security guard's job for free.'

'I'll pay you,' I said immediately. I reached for my wallet. 'How much? 500 rupees?'

He thought for a second, his eyes calculating. 'Hmm... for 1000, I can stand there for a while.'

'Okay, done,' I said without hesitation. I pulled out a 1000 rupee note and handed it to him. 'Now, please, go stand at that exit. Don't let him pass.'

He took the money, shrugged, and walked over to the archway, positioning himself where he could see everyone leaving.

(Good. Now he can't get out this way without a scene.)

I started my search. I moved past the loud shooting galleries, the basketball toss games, the skeeball alleys. I looked under rows of prize counters and behind large arcade machines. No sign of the blue jacket. My heart was pounding. Dev came back from the other side, his face tight with frustration.

'Where did he go? I checked almost every major game. This place is huge,' Dev said, his voice tense.

'We can't lose this chance. We have to find him,' I said, more to myself than to Dev. We were so close.

I stopped and closed my eyes, blocking out the flashing lights and noise.

(Think, Veer... think like him. He's scared. He's trapped in a mall. He knows we know what he looks like, what he's wearing. He can't stay in the open. Where would he go to hide and also change how he looks?... His shoes! We noted his old brown shoes. He would want to get rid of something distinctive. Where do you take off your shoes?...)

My eyes snapped open. 'Dev, follow me. I think I know where he is.'

I led the way, moving quickly through the back of the fun zone toward a brightly lit area filled with the sounds of laughing and bouncing. It was the trampoline park—a vast space of connected trampolines, foam pits, and play structures. Dozens of children were jumping and screaming with joy.

On one side of the trampoline park was a separate, quieter section for smaller children. It had a soft foam floor and a series of small, cube-shaped playrooms made of padded walls and mesh netting. They were like little caves where toddlers could play safely.

I pointed silently to the row of small, dimly lit playrooms. Dev's eyes followed my finger, and they went wide with understanding.

We walked over slowly, trying not to draw attention. We peered into the first few cubes. They were empty or had small children playing. In the very last cube, tucked into the far corner, sitting perfectly still in the shadows, was Bablu. He had taken off his blue jacket and was sitting on it. He was wearing just his t-shirt. And on his feet were the bright red grip socks given out by the trampoline park. His brown shoes were nowhere to be seen.

'How... how did you find me?' Bablu whispered. His voice was full of pure fear and disbelief as he saw us looming in the entrance.

'Yes, sir, I mean how?' Dev asked me, his own face a mix of amazement and relief.

I allowed myself a small, tight smile. 'I knew Bablu was smart. So he would not hide in an open game area where people walk by. Also, Bablu knew that we knew what he was wearing, especially his old brown shoes. They were easy to spot. So he came here, where you have to take off your shoes and wear these special socks. And finally, the whole trampoline park is open, but these little rooms are the only truly hidden spots.'

Dev's jaw dropped. He looked from me to Bablu and back again, impressed.

'Brilliant,' Bablu said softly, almost without thinking. Then he clenched his jaw, angry at himself for giving us the compliment.

I reached into the cube, grabbed his arm firmly, and pulled him out. I turned him around, pulled his arms behind his back, and clicked the handcuffs on his wrists tightly. Then I gave him a light, sharp slap on the back of his head.

'I told you not to run.'

We marched him back through the trampoline park. I grabbed his blue jacket from the cube floor. We walked toward the fun zone exit. The tall man was still standing at the archway, looking a bit awkward but staying in place.

'We found him. Thanks, man, for your honesty. You're still here,' I said as we approached.

'You gave me the money for it... Wait, are those handcuffs?' he asked, his eyes going from the cuffs to Bablu's terrified face. He looked deeply confused.

'You can go back to your kids now. Thank you,' I said with a brief smile, and we walked past him, back into the main mall.

We exited the mall from the main glass doors. The cool night air felt good. Ramu was standing next to his taxi, pacing anxiously. When he saw us walking out with Bablu in cuffs, his whole body sagged with relief, and a big smile broke out on his face.

'Get inside,' I said to Bablu, opening the taxi's back door and guiding him in. Dev got in right beside him, making sure there was no space for escape.

'You found him! Thank God!' Ramu said, his voice full of genuine happiness. 'I saw the other car leave. I was so worried.'

'But, sir, now what?' Dev said, his practical mind already on the next problem. 'We are not safe in Dehradun. That text said there's a meeting tonight. His gang will miss him soon. We have to leave now. And the night trains to Mumbai will be completely full.'

'Yes, you are right,' I said, the urgency settling in my bones. 'I have to call the IG, sir. He's the only one who can help us move fast.'

'Yes, he can cut through any problem,' Dev agreed.

I took out my phone and scrolled to IG's direct number. I took a deep breath and called.

'Hello? Jai Hind, sir,' I said when he answered.

'Jai Hind, Veer. What's happened? It's 9 o'clock at night,' he said. His voice was alert, knowing I wouldn't call at this hour for nothing.

'Sir, I have the man. Bablu. We have him in custody,' I said. I gave him a very quick summary: the club, the chase through the mall, the capture.

There was a short pause on the line. 'Okay, wait. Don't move. Let me do something,' he said, his tone all business, and the line went dead.

'What did he say?' Dev asked immediately.

'He's arranging something for us. We wait,' I replied.

(I should call Mom. She'll be worried.)

'Hello, Mom?' I said when she picked up.

'Veer? Beta, is everything okay?' Her voice was laced with motherly worry.

'Mom, we found him. The case is breaking. We have to go back to Mumbai now,' I said.

'What? So fast? At least come home and show me your face, have a cup of tea before you go!' she pleaded.

'Mom, I want to, but it is too urgent. I have to go. Tell Father, okay? And... where is Mohit?' I asked, the real worry for my brother coming through.

'He is in his room, studying. He came home a while ago,' she replied.

I let out a deep, slow breath I didn't know I was holding. Mohit was home, safe and sound. A huge weight was lifted off my shoulders.

'Okay, Mom. That's good. I will call you as soon as I reach Mumbai,' I promised.

'Okay, beta. Please, take care. Both of you,' she said, and hung up.

Almost exactly five minutes later, my phone rang. It was the IG.

'Listen, Veer,' he said, no pleasantries. 'I have booked you two tickets on the last flight to Mumbai tonight. It leaves in two hours. I have spoken to the airport security chief. He will meet you at a special gate. You will have no checks, no delays. Go straight to the Air India counter. Everything is arranged. Meet me in my office the moment you land.'

'Okay, sir. Thank you, sir. This is a big help,' I said, truly grateful.

'Just get him here safely,' he said, and the call ended.

'Move to the airport, Ramu. Fast, but safe,' I said.

'Okay, sir,' Ramu said. He started the engine and pulled smoothly into the late-night traffic.

For the whole twenty-minute drive to the airport, none of us spoke. Bablu sat between Dev and me, staring straight ahead, his face a blank mask. We asked him no questions. He offered no words. The only sound was the hum of the taxi and the noise of the city outside.

The Dehradun airport was small and quiet at this hour. Ramu pulled up right at the departure gate.

'Here you are, sir,' Ramu said, putting the taxi in park.

We got out. I turned to Ramu. I felt a strong rush of respect for this simple, honest man. I put my hands on his shoulders.

'I don't know how to say this properly,' I began, 'but you are the main reason we caught Bablu. If you had not come forward, if you had not trusted us with what you knew about the police, we would have been blind. We would have had no idea who to trust. You are the real hero in this.'

Ramu's eyes grew shiny. He shook his head. 'No, sir, thank you. Because of you, I feel hope that our Dehradun can become clean again. Just like this, if every member of this gang is caught, I will be the happiest man. You have no idea what this poison is doing to our young people.'

'I promise you,' I said, looking him straight in the eye, 'I will personally talk to the IG about this entire drug network in Dehradun. We will take the strictest action. And now we have Bablu, the main link. The chain will break.'

'Let's go, sir. We need to check in,' Dev said gently, touching my arm. He was right; time was short.

'Yes,' I said. I took my bag and nodded to Dev. We each took one of Bablu's arms and started walking toward the bright lights of the terminal entrance.

As we were about to walk through the automatic doors, I heard Ramu's voice call out loudly behind us, full of emotion: 'Thank you, sir!'

I turned to look back one last time. He was standing by his taxi, holding his old mobile phone. The screen was lit up. He was showing me a text message notification—a bank alert for 10,000 rupees credited to his account. The money I had quietly transferred to him using the phone number he'd given me. It was a small thank you for his bravery, for feeding his family, for being a good man.

I raised my hand high and waved a final goodbye. Then I turned, took a firm grip on Bablu's arm, and walked into the airport, ready to take the final part of this journey back to Mumbai.

CHAPTER SIXTEEN

It's Not What You Think

The flight from Dehradun to Mumbai usually takes about four hours. The plane was quiet, with the soft hum of the engines and the dim cabin lights. After we sat down and the seatbelt sign went off, I took out my phone. I needed to tell Anil something good for once. I typed a quick message.

'We caught him. Bringing him back on a flight now. Now we can find your friends.' I sent it with a thumbs-up emoji. I felt a small relief. At least they would know we were moving forward.

A short while later, the flight announcement came. We had entered the plane and found our seats. I sat on the left aisle seat, Dev sat on the right aisle seat, and Bablu was between us, in the middle seat. There was no way for him to run now. He looked out the small window at the dark sky, his face blank.

Once the plane was in the air, I turned to Bablu. His face was still blank, staring at the seat in front of him.

'Listen, Bablu,' I started, keeping my voice low. 'Tell us everything now. It will be easier for you. The Mumbai police back home know how to get answers. Do you understand what I am saying?'

'I don't want to tell you anything,' Bablu said. He did not look at me.

Out of the corner of my eye, I saw Dev close his eyes. He made his fist very tight. He was controlling his anger.

Then Dev opened his eyes and looked at Bablu. He didn't shout. Instead, he asked a question in a soft voice. 'How is your little brother?'

Bablu's head snapped to look at Dev. His blank face broke. He looked shocked, then stressed. 'Shiva... I will kill you,' he mumbled under his breath.

'Tell me,' Dev continued, still soft. 'What will happen when your brother finds out you are doing these bad things? His heart will break. He is an innocent boy.'

'How do you know I have a brother? How do you know about Shiva?' Bablu asked. His voice was a mix of fear and confusion. 'Only he knows about my brother. He promised me on his life that he would not tell anyone.'

'We are police,' Dev replied simply. 'What did you think?'

Bablu closed his eyes. He was thinking hard. I could see his mind working.

'I can't tell you,' Bablu said finally. He opened his eyes. They were getting wet. 'You guys know only one percent about them. They are so strong. You don't know how many big people are connected to them. Almost the whole country is connected. If I tell you anything, they will destroy me. Completely.'

'How?' I asked, leaning closer.

'They have something... something very important...' He stopped himself. 'Sorry, sir... I can't.' He put his head down and started to cry quietly into his hands.

'Bablu, think about your brother,' I said, keeping my voice firm but not unkind. 'Do you want his life to be easy and happy or not? Tell me.' I waited until he looked up. I gave him direct eye contact. 'I promise you, I will take care of him.'

'What have I done?' he said, crying, his hands on his head.

'Tell us, Bablu,' I said. 'Just like your brother, Sital also has a sister. Think about how she is feeling right now. Only you have an idea of that pain.'

Bablu's head jerked up at the name 'Sital'. His eyes opened wide.

'Okay,' he whispered. He wiped his tears with the back of his hand. 'I will tell you everything. But you have to promise me some things.'

'What things?' I asked.

'After my arrest, no one tells my brother about me. My name is hidden from the news. You give my brother a good education. And in jail, you protect me. That's all I want.' His tone had changed. It was softer, pleading.

'If you tell us everything correctly, and it helps us, then yes, we can do these things for you,' I said.

(Yes! Finally!) I thought. My heart was beating fast. We were getting somewhere.

'No one knows how many people are in the group,' Bablu began, his voice serious and low. 'Are they five, ten, twenty, or just one person? Is he old, young, what is his name, a man or a woman? Nobody knows. The only thing we know is that everyone calls him the MASTER JI.'

'The MASTER JI?' I repeated. The name sent a chill down my back. 'How did you join him?'

'It's not our choice,' Bablu said, shaking his head slowly. 'I had a big debt. Almost twenty lakh rupees. I had nothing to pay for it. So one day, a friend told me about a guy. He took me to him. That guy told me to steal a watch from a house without getting caught. I had to do it in under twenty minutes. If I did it, he would give me a lot of money. I didn't want to do it. But I had no other option except ending my life. But because of my brother, I can do that. He has no one except me. Our parents died very early. So the only option left was this one. I said yes. I stole the watch in under ten minutes. Everyone was shocked. That guy gave me one lakh rupees. But nineteen lakhs were still left. I didn't know what to do. Then, after four days, I got a phone call. The voice said that if I joined him, he would give me the remaining nineteen lakhs. So I said yes. I joined him. After that, I just did what he said. Stole cars, bikes, expensive items.' Bablu looked down at his hands.

'So how did you start with these kidnappings?' Dev asked.

'After the small things, I started liking it. So much money after every job. I made some friends. I bought my dream bike. I was enjoying life. Then he moved me to Group B,' Bablu said.

'Group B?' I said. 'What is that?'

'He divides people into groups,' Bablu explained. 'Group A, Group B, Group C, and Group XE. Group A is people who steal things, fight if needed. They are low-level, beginners. Then comes Group B. They do kidnappings and control Group A. Then comes Group C. They do murders and run the whole drugs, guns, and other businesses. And in the last, Group XE. That is like the MASTER JI. No one knows how they look. They just tell everyone what to do next.'

'That is a big system,' I said, trying to understand it all.

'I told you, sir. You know only one percent,' he said, looking straight into my eyes.

'Okay, now the main question,' Dev said. 'Where are Ajay and Sital?'

Bablu took a deep breath. He started sweating. 'Okay, listen carefully....' He paused and looked around the plane cabin nervously. 'Sorry, Ma'am, I have to tell,' he muttered to himself.

'Who is this 'Ma'am ?' I asked quickly.

'I will tell you everything,' Bablu said, ignoring my question. 'From the very beginning.' Dev and I got ready to listen.

Bablu's Story:

In Mumbai, I worked in a machine shop. It was to show a normal life. Like me, there are many people who work for him but live like normal people. So, on December 16, I was doing my daily cleaning job at the shop. The shop was loud with machine sounds. It was hot and smelled of oil. I was wiping down a big metal press.

'You missed that spot. Where is your brain?' the shop owner shouted at me. He was a fat man who was always angry.

'Oh, sorry, sir. I will clean it,' I said quickly. I took my rag and wiped the spot.

'Do your work properly or find another job,' he said. He walked away, his boots making loud sounds on the floor.

'I don't like him,' my friend Rakesh said from the other side of the room. He was cleaning another machine. He looked tired and dirty.

'To show a normal life and not get caught, we have to work,' I said. I kept my eyes on my work.

'What about today's plan?' Rakesh asked, looking at me.

'Which plan?' I replied. I was confused.

'You don't know? I got a message from a guy in Group C.'

'What message? He didn't message me anything,' I said.

'First, turn ON your game and check,' Rakesh said.

(We did not use normal apps to talk. It was too risky. The police can find those messages. So we used a mobile game. We would send a friend request on the game. Then we would use the game's chat to talk. After talking, we would unfriend each other. This would delete the chat forever from the game.)

I took out my phone. I turned on the game. I saw a friend request from a user named 'DarkHorse21'. I accepted it. There was one message.

(You guys have done good work. We are arranging a party today at 9 PM.)

'See? What do you think?' Rakesh asked. He was smiling.

'No, bro, I don't want to go,' I said.

'Why? What happened?' he asked. His smile went away.

'I'm not having a good feeling. I think it's my stomach,' I said. It was not a full lie. My stomach did feel tight.

'What are you saying, man? After so long, they are giving us a party! You are not coming?' He looked sad and a little angry.

'I want to, but... I'm really not feeling well,' I said.

'Okay, then take care. I'll tell you what happened at the party later.'

'Sounds good,' I said.

Rakesh finished his work after twenty minutes and left the store. The owner came back out from his small office.

'All done?' he asked me.

'Yes, sir. Just one more machine,' I said. I tried to look sick.

'What happened? Any problem?' he said, looking at my face.

'Nothing, sir. Just not feeling good. I think it's my stomach.'

'Oh... Do one thing. Go home and get some rest, okay?' he said. He gave a small smile. He could be kind sometimes.

'Thank you, sir,' I said, smiling back.

'That's okay. Get some rest. Don't come back from tomorrow, always want a holiday. Clean that last machine and close the store. He said with a serious expression, I am going.' Then his face became more serious. 'And where is Rakesh?... Gone again?... I will fire him soon.' He shook his head and left the store, locking the office door from the outside.

I think Rakesh was right, he have to hate him.

I was alone in the big, quiet shop. The machines were silent. (When will this work be over?) I thought. I was tired in my mind, not just my body.

The last machine was very dirty. It took me more than twenty extra minutes to clean it properly. My back was hurting. Just as I was finishing, my phone buzzed. It was a message. It was from Shiva.

My heart felt lighter seeing his name. We chatted for a few minutes. He wanted to meet. We decided to meet at our secret place. After some time, I closed the shop. I took my bike, an old but good bike, and drove to the place.

After thirty minutes, I reached our secret place. It was an old playground in a poor area of the city. A boy had died there a few years ago in an accident. After that, the police closed it for safety. No one played there now. The swings were broken. The slide was rusty. It was all empty and quiet, especially at night.

There, under a broken streetlight, I saw Shiva. He was sitting on a broken bench, his head down.

'Hey, buddy,' I said as I walked over. I sat on the bench next to him. The wood creaked. 'Now tell me exactly what to do.'

'I already told you. Kidnap a boy named Ajay.' Shiva's voice was flat.

'Why? What did he do?'

'Ask what he did not do,' Shiva said, his voice rising with anger. 'He ruined my school life. No one wants to talk to me now because of him. They all laugh at me.'

'Oh, so you want to kidnap him and then what?'

'I want a video of him crying. And I want him to say sorry to me in front of the whole school. On his knees.' He closed his fist so hard his knuckles turned white.

'Cool, bro. I will do that. But he is from your school. That means he probably has good security. His father must be a big man, I guess,' I said, thinking of the problems.

'I don't know what his father does, but yes, he is rich. You have to get him to come out of his house. Kidnap him when no one is around. At night is good.'

'Okay... and when do you want him?' I asked.

'He is with his friends every day except Sunday. On Sunday, he goes for cricket practice alone. No friends go with him. So it is perfect. December 21st, Sunday, is the date,' he replied. He had planned it well.

'After listening, I think you have planned this very hard,' I said. I tried to laugh a little to make it less serious.

'What about money?' Shiva asked, looking at me.

'I told you already. I have stopped these kidnapping jobs. I am doing this last time only because of you. Not for money. You are like my brother. You are the only one who knows about my real brother and who takes care of him. So for that, I can do anything for you for free.'

(Shiva does not know I work for the MASTER JI. He thinks I am just a small-time criminal who does bad things for money. He met me years ago at his school. He had fallen and hurt his leg. I was passing by on my bike. I gave him a lift to the hospital. At the hospital, the police came asking questions about a nearby theft. Shiva, without knowing me, told the police I was with him all day, helping him. He saved me that day. From that day, I have treated him like my second brother. He is the only one I trust with my little brother's safety.)

'Thank you so much, brother,' Shiva said. He leaned over and hugged me tightly. I could feel he was shaking.

Then, suddenly, my phone rang. The loud ringtone broke the quiet of the playground. It was Rakesh, my friend from the shop.

'Where are you? Everyone is asking for you,' he said. His voice sounded urgent.

'I told you already. Why are you not understanding? I am busy,' I said, annoyed.

'There is a problem...' he said, his voice dropping to a whisper.

'What problem?' I said, getting serious,

'Red Meeting,' he said.

The words felt like ice water. A Red Meeting. That was serious. It meant the bosses were angry. I have to go now, the meeting is so important to me.

'Now?' I asked, my stomach dropping.

'Yes. Come fast. And bring your notebook. The meeting is starting soon.'

'I will be there in ten minutes,' I said and hung up the call. My hands were suddenly cold.

'What happened?' Shiva asked, seeing the change in my face.

'I have to go. My friend is calling urgently. Big problem,' I said, standing up.

'Okay, bye. Be safe. I will plan exactly how to kidnap him,' Shiva said. He still sat on the bench, looking small under the dim light.

I nodded, got on my bike, and left the playground in a hurry. The wind was cold on my face as I drove. My mind was racing between Shiva's plan and the fear of the Red Meeting. I did not know then how both these things would come together in a very bad way.

CHAPTER SEVENTEEN

RED MEETING

(The first thing I needed to do was go home and pick up my notebook. The journey took me twenty minutes on my bike through the familiar, winding streets of my neighbourhood. I parked in my usual spot, the sound of the engine fading into the city's constant hum. I entered my apartment building, the air inside cooler and smelling like always, old concrete and cleaning supplies. I fished the keys from my bag, the metal cold against my fingers, and unlocked my door. Inside, my only best friend was waiting for me. He is white with beautiful black stripes—my cat, curled up on the window.)

"How are you, buddy? Did you eat properly?" I asked him, my voice softening.

He can't talk, of course. In response, he simply rotated his tail in that slow, thoughtful way he has and hopped down, padding over to the balcony where his food bowl sat, empty and clean. I felt guilt. I checked the kitchen, opening the old refrigerator. The light flickered for a second before staying on. I took out a half-full bottle of milk, poured some into his clean bowl, and placed it before him. He began lapping it up immediately, a soft, contented sound. I watched him for a moment, this simple creature who asked for nothing but food and a little company.

Then, my mind returning to the task, I went to the bedroom. The room was dim, the curtains drawn. I shifted my heavy bed a few inches to the side, the legs scraping against the tiled floor. Beneath it, almost invisible, was a small floorboard with a faint edge. I pried it up with my fingernails, revealing my secret box—a simple metal container, unremarkable to anyone who might see it. Inside were all my important things: some saved money, a few old letters, and the notebook. I pulled the notebook out, its black cover worn soft at the corners. I placed it carefully in my bag, closed the box, and slid the floorboard back. I stopped in the kitchen, drank a full glass of cool water straight from the tap, and then left again, locking the door behind me.

The location for the Red Meeting was across town in an old, run-down apartment complex. The ride took fifty minutes. I pulled up to the address. The building looked like it was sagging under its own weight, paint peeling in long strips. A poor-looking man was standing outside the rusted metal gate, noisily eating a bag of chips. I got off my bike and walked close to him.

"Open the gate," I said to him, keeping my voice flat.

He didn't look up. "Who are you? I don't know you," he said, continuing to eat.

"Stop playing. You've seen me many times already, going inside with the others," I said, annoyance creeping into my tone.

"Say the code, then," he replied, finally glancing at me, his eyes dull.

"C1218," I said. "Now open the gate."

"That's all I wanted. You know I don't have a personal problem with you, but rules are rules," he said, a thin smile appearing on his face. He wiped his hands on his pants, took out a large ring of keys from his pocket, and unlocked the small metal gate with a loud clang.

I entered the building. The entrance was a tunnel of darkness. I walked straight ahead for what felt like two minutes, my footsteps echoing, until lights flickered on one by one, revealing a long, empty hallway.

"Look who has arrived," a voice called out. A man was leaning against the wall further down, a drink in his hand. He waved the glass toward me. I raised my hand in a brief, silent hello.

Then another man stepped out of a doorway. "They are waiting inside," he said, not smiling. He pointed a thumb toward a heavy door at the end of the hall. A sign on it read 'No Entry' in written in red paint.

I moved towards it and knocked twice. The door was opened not by a handle from my side, but from within. A giant of a man filled the doorway. He must have been nearly seven feet tall, with muscles that strained against his shirt. He looked down at me, his expression changed. "They are waiting for you," he said, stepping aside just enough for me to slip past.

The room was dark, lit only by the glow of a large screen on the far wall.

"You are late. The meeting just started," my friend's voice whispered from the shadows beside me.

"Sorry," I murmured back, giving him a small sign with my hand.

On the big screen, a man with sleek golden glasses was talking. He was addressing our C-ranked leader, who stood respectfully before a camera in our room. The man on the screen had a refined look, but his voice was oddly high and nasal, not matching his powerful appearance.

"How many do you have?" the man on screen asked.

"We have thirty right now," our C-ranked leader replied, his voice steady.

"Why so low?"

"Security is very high now all over the city. It's making collections difficult."

"I don't care about your security problems. I want forty, as per our usual agreement. I am already giving you more money than the other buyers."

"We need time. Please, take the thirty now, and we will arrange the other ten later. We just need a few more days."

"No. I want the full shipment at one time. I can give you extra time if you must have it, but no more than two weeks. That is my final offer."

Our leader said with his head slightly. "Thank you, sir, for giving us the time."

"Okay, but mark my words, this is the last extension. After this, I will take my complaints directly to MASTER JI. You do not want that."

A chill went through the room at the name. "That time will never come, sir. You will have your forty," our leader said quickly.

"Now, show me what you have ready today. Let me see them."

"We have twenty men and ten women. Among the men, thirteen are above the age of eighteen and seven are below. Among the women, seven are above eighteen, and three are below."

(Yes, this is what they call the Red Meeting. I don't think I need to explain to you what this business is—the buying and selling of people. A deep sickness settled in my stomach, as it always did.)

"That's a good mix," the man on the screen said, a note of pleasure in his mismatched voice.

"I knew you would appreciate it. Bablu, bring them in here," the C-ranked man said, turning and pointing at me.

"Yes, sir," I said. I turned and gave a signal to the men waiting by the back door.

They filed in, a single line of misery. Their hands were bound, and their eyes were blindfolded with rough cloth. Soft crying and sniffling filled the room. They looked so young, so scared.

"Perfect!" the man on the screen said, sounding genuinely excited. "A very good selection. Healthy, young. Yes, this will do."

"I am glad you are satisfied, sir."

"After two weeks, send the full forty as arranged. My men will be waiting for you at the usual port. Do not be late." Without another word, the screen went black.

The main lights in the room buzzed and flickered on, very bright. We all blinked, seeing each other's faces clearly now in the light.

"Take them back to the holding cells. Gently," I instructed the guards. They led the crying line away.

The C-ranked man walked over to me, his face changed. "You were late today."

"Sorry, Bhaiya," I said, using the respectful term. "It won't happen again."

"You heard what he said. Ten more people before two weeks are over. We have a mountain of work to do. I don't need anyone slacking," he said, his eyes boring into mine. Then he turned and left the room, his footsteps echoing.

My friend came up beside me. "Bro... getting ten more people in just two weeks is nearly impossible. The police are everywhere after those last few disappearances made the news."

"Yes... You are right," I said, sinking down onto a worn-out sofa. The weight of it felt crushing.

"Here, have a drink. You look like you need it." He handed me a glass of something strong. I took it and drank, the liquid burning a path down my throat, doing nothing to warm the cold feeling inside.

We talked about other things for the next forty minutes—sports, a new movie, anything to avoid the subject of the ten people we needed to find. After a while, I stood up. "I'm heading out."

"Stay safe," my friend said.

I left the building, the night air feeling no fresher than the air inside. I rode my bike home on autopilot, my mind a whirl of numbers and faces.

I don't even remember the ride home or when I finally fell asleep. I woke up the next day with the sun already high, my head aching from yesterday's drink. I dragged myself out of bed. My cat meowed from the doorway. I made a simple meal from some old bread and the last two eggs, scrambling them together. I ate half and put the other half in his bowl. He purred loudly, rubbing against my legs. I took a long, cold shower, trying to wash away the laziness, but it never worked.

Afterwards, I turned on the small TV in the living room. The news was on, as it always was. A serious-faced reporter was talking about the rising number of missing persons in the city, showing blurred photos of smiling faces. I turned it off. The silence was worse.

Suddenly, my phone rang. The screen said 'Private Number.' A knot tightened in my chest.

"Hello? Who is this?" I said, unable to hide a yawn born of exhaustion, not sleep.

"Bablu." The voice was low, calm, and carried an unnatural weight. "I am an assistant of MASTER JI."

I literally jumped from the sofa, my heart hammering against my ribs. My cat is scared and goes under the furniture.

"De... Dem... MASTER JI's assistant?" I stammered, my mouth dry. "I... I think I am the first one to ever hear the voice of one of you guys."

"Keep quiet and listen carefully. I have sent you something. It will arrive at your door in five minutes. Open it. Inside, you will find photographs. MASTER JI has a specific request. He wants only these two people. We have chosen you for this task because we believe you are the only one in your circle capable of doing it cleanly."

The words were like ice water. "Okay. What... what are their names?" I managed to ask.

"They are written on the backs of the photos. We want them delivered by tomorrow night—Friday. If you succeed, we are strongly considering a promotion for you. Bring them to the address provided in the package." His tone left no room for questions.

A promotion. Group C..... The thought was terrifying and thrilling all at once. "Thank you... Thank you for giving me this opportunity."

"Hmm. And this phone number will be destroyed immediately after this call. We will contact you again from a different number when necessary." The line went dead with a soft click.

I stood frozen in the middle of my living room for a full minute. Then I rushed to the window, peering down at the street. Five minutes felt like an hour. Finally, a delivery scooter pulled up. A man in a uniform got off with a small, plain cardboard box.

My doorbell rang. I ran to the gate and opened it.

"Parcel for you, sir," the delivery man said, not making eye contact. He held out a digital clipboard. "Sign here, please."

"Yes," I said, scribbling a meaningless signature. I took the box, closed the gate, and carried it to my room as if it were a bomb.

With careful, trembling fingers, I opened the box. Inside, resting on a bed of plain paper shreds, were two color photographs. One was of a young man in his early twenties, handsome, with a confident smile. The other was of a young woman, perhaps a little younger, with intelligent eyes. I turned them over. On the back of the man's photo, written in neat block letters: AJAY. On the woman's: SITAL.

A small, folded note was underneath them. I unfolded it.

"Hello Bablu,

We hope you will execute this work with your usual efficiency. You have been given two photographs—one male, one female. You are to acquire them both.

Ajay will leave his residence at approximately 7:50 PM. He will go to the MT building (the old commercial complex on the north side) and will wait there alone. This is your window. No one else is there at that time.

Several hours later, Sital will pass by the same location. You can acquire her there as well.

Bring both assets to the JJ Club by midnight.

Your advance payment of 10 lakh rupees is included in the box.

- D.E.M.O.N"

TEN lakhs. Just as an advance. My hands shook as I lifted the shreds of paper. Beneath them were bundles of cash, neatly stacked. This was more money than I usually saw for a whole job. These people were clearly very, very important to someone high up.

I took the money and locked it in my small wall safe. Then my mind, trained by necessity, switched to planning mode. How to approach him? Where to put his vehicle after the kidnapping? What about witnesses?

Then, a lightning bolt of recognition struck me. Ajay. This was the same Ajay that my school friend Shiva had been complaining about! The one he wanted to teach a lesson.

I immediately grabbed my phone and called Shiva. He picked up after a few rings.

"Hello, Shiva?" I said, trying to sound normal.

"Yes, bro! I was just about to call you," he said, his voice sounding chilled.

"Why? What's happened?"

"Listen, about that plan... forget it. Don't kidnap Ajay."

"Why?" I asked, playing confused. "I thought you wanted to scare him."

"I did... but I thought about it all last night. I really don't like this plan anymore. What if he figures it out? What if he tells his father? I could be kicked out of school, or worse. My family... I can't risk it. Sorry, bro, just drop the whole idea, okay?" He sounded genuinely scared.

(It was better this way. Better he knew nothing about this real, far more dangerous operation.) "Okay, bro. No problem. Your call," I said, feigning mild disappointment.

"Thank you, bro. Really. By the way, why were you calling me?"

"Oh, nothing important. I just wanted to talk about this Ajay plan, but it's okay. Since you've changed your mind, no worries. Talk later, bye." I hung up before he could ask more questions.

A grim smile touched my lips. Now the path was clear. MASTER JI's men wanted Ajay, and Shiva was out of the picture. It was perfect.

But I couldn't do this alone. Two targets, a tight schedule, and the high stakes—it required a partner. I called my friend from the meeting.

"Come to my place. Now. It's urgent."

Fifteen minutes later, he was at my door, breathing slightly heavily. "What's happening? You look pale."

I showed him the photos, the note, and the money. I told him about the call. His eyes widened with a mix of fear and greed.

"I can't do this alone," I said finally, my voice quiet.

He was silent for a long moment, staring at Ajay's photo. Then he sighed, a heavy, decisive sound. "Hmm... okay. I will help you. You are like my brother. We look out for each other." He gave my shoulder a firm.

We spent the next few hours planning. We went over every detail, every possible problem. We would need a car, fake plates, chloroform, and masks. We decided on roles, backup plans, and escape routes. By the time he left, we had a solid, if terrifying, plan. We would get everything ready and meet tomorrow.

The next day was the day. I woke up feeling a strange. I did some half-hearted exercises, more out of habit than anything, then got dressed in dark, ordinary clothes. I went to my friend's house, where we kept an old, unremarkable sedan for jobs like this. I let myself in.

"Fake number plates?" I asked.

"Changed last night" he said, pointing to the car outside.

"Our masks?"

"In the glove box."

"Chloroform and rags?"

"Ready in the backseat, in the black bag."

"Good."

"Now we have to wait," I said, but a deep nervousness was beginning in my gut.

"When he arrives," my friend starts telling the plan, "you go up to him, ask for directions or something. Get him to turn around. Put the cloth on his face. I'll pull the car up the second you move. We load him in, and we're gone in sixty seconds."

"Yes," I nodded. "Then I'll drive the car to the first drop point. You take his bike and ditch it in the river like we talked about. Leave no trace."

"Perfect. Then we come back and wait for the girl. We do the same thing for her. We take her when she's alone."

"We should go to the shop first, for our normal shift," I said. "If we don't show up at all, the owner will get suspicious and might come looking or ask questions."

"You're right. Let's go. It's almost time. That old man will skin us alive if we're late."

We took my bike and rode to the small mechanic shop where we worked part-time. The owner, a perpetually angry man, yelled at us for being two minutes late. We put on our gloves and started the mindless work—changing oil, tightening bolts. It was a strange. Doing work and thinking about the plan,

Time passed very slowly. My nervousness grew into a tight ball in my chest. I'd done this many times before, part of the regular collections for the Red Meeting. But this was different. This was a direct order from the very top. The margin for error was zero.

Finally, the clock on the wall showed 7:00 PM. I caught my friend's eye and gave a sharp nod. We started cleaning up.

"Wait! Where do you think you're going? Your shift isn't over for another hour!" the owner barked, wiping his hands on a rag.

"Boss, please," I said, putting on my most apologetic face. "It's his best friend's wedding today. We promised we'd be there on time. You know how these things are."

"Fools! Always trying to sneak away early. Fine! Go! But tomorrow, you both do the full day plus the garage cleanup. No arguments!"

"Thank you,boss! Thank you!" we said, already pulling off our gloves.

We rushed out and onto my bike, weaving through the evening traffic to my friend's house. The car was ready. We quickly put on the fake plates, checked the supplies one last time, and pulled on our plain black masks, stuffing them into our pockets for now. We got into the car, the interior smelling of old vinyl and anxiety.

"MT building. Let's go."

The drive took twenty minutes. The MT building was an old, mostly abandoned commercial complex on the northern edge of the city. At night, it was a ghost town. We parked our car in the shadows of a side street about a hundred meters away, with a clear view of the main entrance. The street was quiet, just the distant sound of traffic and the buzz of a lone streetlight.

"It's 7:48. He should be here any second," my friend whispered, as if someone could hear us.

"I don't see anyone," I said, my fingers tapping nervously on the steering wheel.

Then, right at 7:50, the low rumble of a motorcycle engine cut through the silence. A sleek bike pulled up in front of the main steps of the MT building. A young man in a jacket got off, took off his helmet, and looked around. It was him. Ajay. He checked his phone, then leaned against his bike, waiting.

"That's him. Okay, I'm going," I said, my mouth dry. I pulled the mask over my face and got out of the car, leaving the door slightly open. I walked calmly, trying to look like just a guy out for a walk. I approached him.

"Hello, brother," I said, my voice muffled slightly by the mask.

He turned, a polite but slightly wary look on his face. "Yes? How can I help you?" Up close, he looked even younger than in his photo.

"Actually, I'm a bit lost. Can you tell me where the Shiv Mandir is from here? The big one."

His face relaxed. "Oh, Shiv Mandir? Sure. You go straight down this road for about a kilometer. Then you take a left at the signal with the broken light. Go straight again for maybe five hundred meters, and you'll see it on your right. You can't miss it."

"Which side is the left?" I asked, squinting as if confused. "From this direction?"

"Right here," he said, turning fully to point back the way he had come. "You see where that faded billboard is? That's the turn."

The moment his back was to me, I moved. In one swift motion, I pulled the chloroform-soaked rag from my pocket and clamped it over his nose and mouth. His eyes went wide with shock and terror. He made a muffled sound, and his hands came up, clawing at my arm. He was stronger than I expected. We struggled for a few seconds, him twisting, me holding on with all my strength, the sweet, chemical smell filling the air. Then his muscles went slack, and he slumped to the ground, unconscious.

I looked up. My friend was already there, the car rolling silently to a stop beside us. We worked quickly, opening the back door, lifting Ajay's limp body, and sliding him onto the floor of the backseat. I threw an old blanket over him.

"Go! Now! The bike!" I hissed.

My friend was already on Ajay's motorcycle. He kick-started and started moving, heading towards the river. I got into the driver's seat of the car, my heart pounding so hard I could feel it in my ears. I drove slowly, calmly, away from the MT building, turning into the pre-planned route to our first hiding spot—a locked garage we rented under a fake name a few miles away.

One down.

I parked in the garage, closed the door, and sat in the dark, listening to my own breathing. After about thirty minutes, there was a soft knock on the side door. It was my friend, on foot, slightly out of breath.

"Done," he said, slipping into the passenger seat. "The Bike is at the bottom of the river. No one saw me."

"Good. Now we wait for the second one."

We drove back to our observation spot near the MT building. The street was still deserted. An hour crawled by. I found myself nervously biting my fingernails, a habit I thought I'd broken. Where was she?

Then, just after 9:30 PM, a yellow taxi pulled up to the same spot. A young woman got out, paid the driver, and the taxi didn't leave immediately. She stood there, and the driver seemed to be talking to her through the window.

"What! A taxi?" my friend muttered, dismayed.

"He's just dropping her off... but why isn't he leaving?" I whispered back, my stomach clenching.

For five agonizing minutes. Finally, it pulled away, its taillights disappearing around a corner. She was alone now, looking at her phone, occasionally glancing up the empty street. She was Sital.

"Same plan. You go this time," I told my friend. "I'll bring the car."

He nodded, pulled his mask on, and got out. He walked towards her with a casual slouch. I started the car and began to creep forward, keeping my lights off.

I watched as he approached her. She took a step back immediately, defensive.

"Hello?" he said.

"Who are you? Stay away from me!" she said, her voice sharp with fear.

"No, please, don't be scared. I'm just lost. I'm looking for the Shiv Mandir. Can you help?" His voice was calm, pleading.

I saw her hesitate. "Shiv Mandir? It's... you go straight down this road..." She, too, turned to point, gesturing into the darkness.

It was the moment. He moved fast. The rag was over her face before she could scream. She jerked violently, her purse falling to the ground. Her struggle was shorter. In seconds, she went limp. My friend caught her as she fell. I pulled the car right up beside them. We bundled her into the backseat next to the still-unconscious Ajay, covered them both with the blanket, and picked up her fallen purse.

"Finally. All done," my friend gasped, slumping into the seat as we moved away. He was sweating.

"Now to the JJ Club. Don't speed. Just drive normally," I said, though every nerve was screaming to go faster.

The drive to the JJ Club took forty minutes. The club was in a flashy part of town, all neon lights and expensive cars. We pulled into the parking lot. A man in a dark suit was standing near the entrance, talking into a phone. He saw our car and pointed firmly toward the back of the building.

We followed his silent direction, driving around to the rear where the dumpsters and delivery entrances were. Three identical black SUVs with tinted windows were parked there. As we stopped, a man got out of the middle SUV. He was big, with a blank, professional expression. He walked to my window. I rolled it down.

"Where are they?" he asked, his voice flat.

"In the back," I said.

He leaned down and looked through the rear window, nodding once. "Okay. The boss wants to see you. Get out. Go to the third car."

My friend and I exchanged a glance. We got out of our car. I walked to the third black SUV, my legs feeling like jelly. I knocked softly on the dark window.

It rolled down just a crack, no more than an inch. The interior was pitch black.

"Good work." The voice from inside was smooth, older, and carried absolute authority. It was the same voice from the phone—MASTER JI's assistant. "The remaining payment has been transferred to your usual account"

" And take this..." A female voice came

A hand emerged from the front seat and passed me a large, sealed envelope. I took it.

"Open it later. Inside, you will find two plane tickets to Dehradun and a key. The key is for a car that will be waiting for you at the Dehradun airport parking lot, space number forty-seven," she said.

I was confused. "Dehradun? Mam, I don't"

"You are not safe in this city anymore. The targets were... high-profile. There will be heat. Go to Dehradun with your friend. Lie low for a few months. Destroy your current phone, your SIM card, and everything linked to this identity. Wait for our next command. Consider this a test of your discretion and loyalty." The voice paused. "You have done well. You are now officially a member of Group C. Welcome," she said

A promotion. Just like he'd promised. A laugh came from the dark car—a dry, humourless sound. I forced myself to laugh too, a shaky, nervous echo.

"Thank you so much, ma'am. We won't let you down."

"See that you don't. The plane leaves at 6 AM. Don't miss it."

The window slid up silently. The conversation was over.

I walked back to our car, where my friend was waiting, his eyes wide with questions. The women by the SUVs waved a hand, and two other men emerged and began transferring Ajay and Sital from our car to one of the black SUVs. They handled the unconscious bodies with efficient, impersonal care.

"Let's go," I said to my friend. We got into our now-empty car and drove away, leaving the JJ Club and its dark secrets behind.

I didn't open the envelope until we were back at my apartment. Inside were two first-class tickets in fake names for a flight to Dehradun at dawn, and a single car key with a tag that read 'Lot 47'. My friend stared at the tickets, then at me.

"Group C," he whispered, a strange light in his eyes. It was fear, but underneath, there was pride.

I looked at the key in my hand, then at the photo of my cat, who was sleeping peacefully on the sofa. What am I doing with my life? The thought was clear and terrible. But it was followed by another, colder one: I am surviving.

We had a flight to catch.

CHAPTER EIGHTEEN

Getting Worse

"That's all, sir," Bablu said, finishing his terrible story.

Dev and I sat in stunned silence, our hands pressed to our own heads as if to contain the horror. I was in a state of complete shock, my mind struggling to process the cold, detailed confession of kidnapping and trafficking.

"Those innocent kids," Dev whispered, his voice thick with emotion. His eyes were red, glistening with tears of anger and sorrow. He suddenly slammed his fist down on the armrest between us. "You... you people are not human! You are monsters!" he shouted, unable to contain his rage.

A woman in the seat ahead of us turned around, looking annoyed. "Please, sir, talk softly. Some of us are trying to sleep."

"Sorry, ma'am," Dev mumbled, shrinking back into his seat.

Bablu kept his head down, staring at his cuffed hands. "Yes. I know I did something so bad to others. Unforgivable things. But... just leave it. There's no excuse. Just throw me in jail. That's what I deserve."

His words are emotional. My own mind was racing, piecing together the timeline.

"The Red Meeting..." I said, closing my eyes as the full picture snapped into a horrific focus. "Your friend mentioned that the meeting where you needed ten more people was happening today. That means... Ajay and Sital. They could be part of that shipment right now!" A bolt of adrenaline shot through me.

"Oh, god! You're right!" Dev said, one hand flying back to his head. "We have to go back to Dehradun! We have to intercept that meeting!"

"NO," Bablu said, his voice firm, cutting through our panic.

I turned to him, confused. "What do you mean, 'no'?"

"They are not in the Red Meeting," he stated silently.

"What?!" Dev said, leaning forward to make direct eye contact with Bablu. "You just told us you kidnapped both of them, and then your boss said you needed ten extra people in two weeks. It makes sense! You handed them over, and they became part of the count!"

"Yes, that's what I thought, too. At first," Bablu admitted, his tone weary. "But after we delivered them to the club, my job was done. A few days ago, I got word from my contact that the full forty people for the Red Meeting had finally been collected. My friend and I went to the warehouse to check the final shipment before delivery—standard procedure to make sure there were no problems. We counted them, checked the list... Ajay and Sital were not there. They were not among the ten new people kidnapped to complete the order. I don't know where they went after the JJ Club."

His words landed like physical blows. The one thread we had just pulled—the connection to the trafficking ring—seemed to snap.

"What?" I breathed. "So where did they take them?"

"Sir, I am telling you the truth, I swear on my brother's life. I don't know where they are. Once we handed them over to the men in the black cars, they were out of my world. They were for MASTER JI. Not for the regular market."

"Shit!" Dev said, running his hands through his hair in frustration.

A heavy, hopeless silence descended upon the three of us for the rest of the flight. For forty minutes, no one spoke. I stared at the seatback in front of me, but I wasn't seeing it. My mind was a storm of terrible scenarios.

Bablu is the kidnapper, but he's become a dead end. He doesn't know their final destination. What do I do now? What do I tell their parents? And Anil... oh, Anil. I promised him.

The pilot's voice finally crackled through the cabin, breaking the awful quiet. "Ladies and gentlemen, welcome to Chhatrapati Shivaji Maharaj International Airport, Mumbai. The local time is 8:30 AM, and the outside temperature is a pleasant 23 degrees Celsius."

I checked my watch, doing the mental math. This is the EIGHTH day since they went missing.

As the plane taxied to the gate, I leaned close to Bablu, my voice a low, urgent command. "Listen carefully. You hold my hand tight when we walk out. Do not let go. And where are your mask and your glasses? Put them on now. There will be police waiting, but we need to move you quietly."

He fumbled with the items in his pocket, putting on the large sunglasses and pulling the surgical black mask over his face. We began moving through the jet bridge into the terminal.

We had only taken a few steps into the full, crowded hall when we saw it. The scene ahead was not the normal flow of passengers. It was a solid wall of people, noise, and blinding camera lights. A huge crowd was packed behind the barriers, waving banners that read 'FIND AJAY & SITAL' and 'JUSTICE FOR THE MISSING'. Dozens of reporters and camera crews were searching for positions, their lenses pointed straight at the arriving passengers.

"WHAT IS THIS?!" Bablu whispered harshly, his grip tightening on my arm in panic.

"How... how did this get out?" I muttered, my own heart sinking. This was a disaster.

Before we could even process it, a group of eight police officers in uniform spotted us and began running towards our position, cutting through the crowd.

A young constable reached us first, speaking quickly under his breath. "Inspector, the front exit is not safe. It's a mob. We have to move to the back service gate. Now. Follow me."

"What is going on? Who alerted the media?" I demanded as we broke into a jog, weaving through startled travelers.

The constable just shook his head, gesturing for us to move faster. "No time, sir. This way!"

We followed him through a 'Staff Only' door, down a stark concrete corridor, and out a heavy metal door that led to the service and delivery area behind the airport. Two armored police vans were there, surrounded by at least ten more armed constables who stood alert, their eyes scanning the area.

We sprinted the last few meters. I pushed Bablu into the back of the first van and climbed in after him, with Dev jumping in right behind. The doors slammed shut, and the van pulled away.

Inside the dim, stuffy interior, I finally caught my breath. “What is going on here? Will someone please tell me?” I said, my confusion quickly turning to anger.

The driver, an older head constable, glanced at me in the rearview mirror. “It’s all over the news, sir. All over Mumbai. Since early this morning.”

“How?” Dev asked, confused. “How do they know about Bablu? About the kidnapping? We kept it sealed!”

Suddenly, I pulled out my personal phone. The screen showed ten missed calls and a torrent of message notifications. I opened the messaging app, and the first one made my blood run cold.

It was from Anil. ‘Sir, I am so sorry. I tried my best, but the pressure... my classmates... they wouldn’t stop asking. Someone talked to a reporter. It’s all out. I’m so sorry.’

“SHIT!” I screamed, the word tearing out of me as I slammed my palm against the van’s metal wall. The loud bang echoed in the small space.

“What happened, sir?” Dev asked nervously.

“Anil,” I said, the word heavy with defeat. I lowered my head into my hands. “The classmates. Someone talked.”

Dev let out a long sigh, putting his own hands on his head. “Oh, no... This is the worst thing that could have happened.”

I scrolled through the other messages. Colleagues, superiors, and even a few unknown numbers. Then I saw one that was from the IG himself.

‘Veer. Come directly to me. Do not go to the station first.’

The driver confirmed it. “We are taking the prisoner to the high-security lockup at the headquarters. And IG Sir has ordered that you and Sub-Inspector Dev be brought straight to his office."

"Yes," I said dully, showing Dev the phone. "I just read it."

"This is bad. So, so bad," Dev kept repeating, staring out the tinted window at the city blurring past.

Needing to see the damage for myself, I opened a news app on my phone. The headlines were everywhere: 'MUMBAI KIDNAPPING: MAFIA LINK SUSPECTED', 'BABLU: THE FACE OF EVIL?', 'POLICE CLUELESS IN SEARCH FOR MISSING DUO'.

I switched to a video news site. Every major channel had a live panel or a reporter standing outside the airport or the police station. I clicked on one.

A sharply dressed reporter was speaking directly to the camera. "...and sources within the police are suggesting that the prime suspect, a man known as Bablu, may have already murdered the missing college students and disposed of their bodies in a river. The police have yet to confirm..."

"What?!" I exploded. "They're reporting murder now? With no evidence?!" I switched to another channel.

Here, a reporter was interviewing a man who looked like a local shopkeeper. "Who is this Bablu?" the reporter asked.

The man puffed out his chest for the camera. "He is a big mafia man in Mumbai! A goonda! I have heard he has killed many people since he was just fifteen years old! The police are afraid of him!"

I threw my phone onto the seat next to me in disgust. "What is going on with the news? They're just inventing nonsense! Trial by media!" I hit the seat three times in frustration.

"But how do they even know Bablu's name?" Dev asked a logical question amidst the chaos.

"They are the media, Dev. They have sources everywhere. They pay for information, they lean on people. Someone talked, and now they have a name, and they're building a whole drama around it." I put my hands over my eyes, the weight of the situation crushing me. "This is exactly what I didn't want. This kind of publicity can spook the real culprits, it puts pressure on us to make quick, wrong moves, and it terrifies the families even more."

After twenty more minutes of tense silence, the van pulled into the secure underground parking of the police headquarters. As the driver came to a stop, I turned to the officers in the front.

"Drive him safely to the high-security block. I don't want him to run, and I don't want anyone getting to him. Is that clear?"

"Yes, sir," he said.

Dev and I got out and made our way to the IG's office. The usual respectful hush of the headquarters felt charged, like the calm before a storm. I knocked on the heavy wooden door.

"Come in," a stern voice called.

We entered. "Jai Hind, sir," I said, saluting.

IG sir did not return the salute. He was standing behind his desk, his face like thunder. He picked up a thick file and slammed it back down on the polished wood. "Veer! What in the name of all that is holy is going on? Who told the media? The whole city is screaming for our heads!"

"Sir, it was the victims' classmates. One of them spoke to a reporter. We had a source close to them trying to manage things, but the pressure was too much."

"Is the prisoner secure? Has he confessed?"

"Yes, sir. He is secure. And he has confessed to the kidnapping."

The IG's shoulders relaxed slightly, but then tensed again as he caught my expression. "Then why do you look like you've seen a ghost? We have the kidnapper. We find the kids."

"Sir, he confessed to kidnapping them, but he doesn't know where they are now."

IG sir stared at me as if I were speaking a different language. "What does that mean?"

"Sir, this case... it is much bigger than we thought. It's not a simple ransom kidnapping. It's connected to an organized trafficking ring. And above that, it's connected to a figure they call 'MASTER JI.' Bablu handed them over to MASTER JI's men, but after that, they disappeared into a different channel. He doesn't know their final destination."

The IG sank into his chair, a deep frown etching his face. "Hmm. I see. This is...a problem. Veer, I am under immense pressure. From the government, from the media, from the public. There are... orders."

A cold trickle of fear went down my spine. "What orders, sir?"

"You have already had nine days. Nine days, and the case is not only unsolved, but it has also exploded into a media circus. The decision has been made. The case is being transferred to another team."

"No, sir! Please!" The plea was out of my mouth before I could stop it. I stepped forward, my hands on his desk. "I have to solve this case. I can solve it. I'm closer than anyone! I know the threads, I have the kidnapper talking! Please, sir, you know me."

"I know you, Veer. And I know you are a good officer. But this is not in my hands anymore. You have been given more than enough time."

"Sir, I just need—" I was begging, and I hated the sound of it.

A smooth, familiar voice cut me off from the doorway. "Just like you needed more time on your previous missing case?"

I didn't need to turn around to know who it was. The voice alone made him known. I turned slowly.

It was Inspector Yug. Tall, impeccably dressed, with a permanently smug expression. The officer I disliked more than anyone else in the force.

"The innocent three-year-old girl," he added, coming into the room without being invited. "How much time did you need for that one, Veer? And what was the result again?"

"Who gave you permission to come in here?" I said, my composure breaking.

"He has been given the case," IG said quietly, unable to meet my eyes.

"WHAT? Sir, please! Just give me one more week! Just one! I will solve it!" My voice was loud in the quiet office.

The IG looked from my desperate face to Yug's confident smirk. He let out a long, weary sigh. He was a practical man, caught between loyalty and pressure. "Alright. One week. That is the absolute last chance, Veer. If you do not have the victims found and the main orchestrator in custody in seven days, the case file goes to Inspector Yug's desk. Is that understood?"

It was a lifeline, thin and frayed, but it was all I had. "Thank you, sir. Thank you so much."

"Take one week or one month, you will not be able to solve it," Yug said, a laugh bubbling under his words. "Some officers are just not cut out for certain types of work."

Rage, hot and pure, flooded me. I took a step towards him. "This time, I will show you. I will show everyone."

"Okay, that's enough!" the IG barked, standing up. The authority in his voice pulled us both back. "Veer, we have a press conference in ten minutes. We have to address this media firestorm. Dev, you come with us."

As we turned to leave, the IG stopped me with a hand on my arm. He lowered his voice. "And Veer, listen carefully. At the press conference, you do not tell them that Bablu doesn't know where the kids are. You tell them he is in custody and is not cooperating. He is not opening his mouth. Do you understand? We cannot show weakness or ignorance to the public right now. We must appear in control."

I understood the politics of it, even though it sickened me. I nodded. "Yes, sir."

The press conference room was a spectacle of noise and light. It was packed wall-to-wall with reporters, photographers, and camera operators. The air hummed with tension and the heat of the lights. We took our seats on the small stage behind a long table covered with microphones.

IG stepped up to the podium, and a hush fell over the room.

"Thank you for coming," he began, his voice amplified and echoing. "We have a significant update. Last night, our team successfully apprehended the prime suspect in the kidnapping of Ajay and Sital. His name is Bablu."

A wave of excited chatter swept through the room. Cameras flashed.

A reporter immediately shouted a question. "So, have you solved the case? Are the students safe?"

The IG's face remained grave. "Not yet."

The room erupted. The calm vanished. Dozens of reporters leapt to their feet, shouting over one another.

"What do you mean?!"

"Is Bablu not the culprit?!"

"Where are Ajay and Sital?!"

"Tell us properly!"

The IG raised his hands, calling for order. "Please! Silence! One question at a time!"

The noise slowly died down to a restless murmur.

A senior female reporter stood. "Inspector General, what do you mean by 'not yet'? You have the kidnapper."

"We have the man who physically took them, yes. But he is not cooperating with the investigation. He is not telling us the location of the victims."

Another roar of questions. "Where are they?" "Is he working alone?" "What are his demands?"

The IG pointed to a journalist he recognised. "One question."

The man stood. "My question is for Inspector Veer singh."

My heart thudded. The IG gestured for me to come forward. I stood, my legs feeling unsteady, and walked to the podium. He handed me a microphone and returned to his seat.

"Yes?" I said, my voice sounding calmer than I felt.

The reporter, a man with sharp eyes, didn't smile. "Inspector Veer, we are aware of your record. We know you have struggled with missing persons cases in the past. We all remember what happened with the three-year-old girl two years ago. The case that went cold. What makes you think this will be different?"

His words were a punch to the gut. For a full twenty seconds, I said nothing. The room was utterly silent, waiting. In my mind, I saw her face—the little girl from that old case. The one I couldn't bring home. The failure that haunted me every night.

I swallowed hard, pushing the image away. I leaned into the microphone. "I promise you," I said, my voice low but clear, carrying across the silent room, "that mistake will not happen again. I will solve this case. We will bring Ajay and Sital home."

The reporter gave a slight nod. "I admire your confidence, Inspector."

"Okay, that is all for now," IG said quickly, stepping back to the podium. "We have an active investigation to run."

The room exploded again with shouted questions, but we were already moving off the stage, flanked by constables, leaving the chaos behind.

Outside the room, in the relative quiet of the corridor, the IG turned to me. "Go to the police headquarters. Work fast. The clock is ticking louder than ever."

"Yes, sir," I said. Dev and I took a police jeep and began the drive to our police headquarters.

"The whole thing is a mess," Dev said, slumping in his seat. "A complete mess."

"Yes, Dev. And now the IG has given me a final deadline. One week. After that, Yug gets the case, and we become a footnote." I couldn't keep the dejection from my voice.

"No, sir! That cannot happen!" Dev said, suddenly sitting up straight, his determination reigniting. "We have to solve this, at any cost!"

"But how?" I asked, the frustration boiling over. "We don't know where they are! We only know that some mythical 'MASTER JI' has them. A ghost. No one has seen him, no one knows what he looks like, where he lives, his real name... nothing. Bablu is a dead-end."

"Then we have to make that dead end talk some more," Dev said, his mind racing. "We have to push him harder. Maybe if he thinks harder, he'll remember a detail—a phrase he heard, a partial license plate, a glimpse of someone. If he feels the pressure is on him now, maybe he'll give up something important to save himself."

He had a point. Extreme pressure sometimes cracked memories open.

"Yes," I agreed. "And thank you, Dev. Seriously. But speaking of pressure, how did you know about Bablu having a younger brother? When did Shiva tell you that? That was the key that broke him."

Dev looked at me, and a strange, slightly sheepish smile spread across his face. "Just like you, sir, I also had no idea Bablu had a little brother."

I stared at him. "What?"

"And Shiva never told me anything about a brother. Not a word."

I was completely lost. "So... all of that? The way you confronted him, the specific detail... that was all a..."

"A guess," Dev finished, his smile widening. "An educated bluff. I read about it in a psychology book on interrogation. You act like you know a devastating personal secret about the suspect. You present it as an absolute fact. If your guess is wrong, they just get confused and deny it, and you move on. But if, by chance, your guess is correct... it shatters their world. It makes them believe you know everything, that resistance is useless. So they talk."

The sheer audacity of it left me speechless. I replayed the scene on the plane—Dev's confident, accusing tone. "So all of that... his entire confession... came because of a guess?"

Dev nodded, still smiling. "See? It was correct."

For a moment, the immense stress of the day cracked. A disbelieving laugh escaped my lips. Then Dev started laughing too. In the middle of the terrible pressure, the media storm, and the looming deadline, we sat in that jeep and laughed until our sides hurt. It was a release of pure, shocked relief.

After a few minutes, our laughter subsided, fading back into the grim reality around us. The jeep turned onto the familiar street leading to our station.

I looked at Dev, my partner. "We have to find them, Dev. We have to."

He looked out the window at the city rushing past, his face set in a mask of resolve. He nodded once, firmly. "We will, sir."

CHAPTER NINETEEN

LAST CHANCE

It took us twenty minutes to reach the police headquarters from the IG's office. The drive was tense and quiet, both of us lost in our own thoughts about the impossible week ahead.

As soon as we entered the busy station, I called out to the nearest constable. "Where is Bablu?"

"Inside the high-security interrogation room, sir," the young officer replied, pointing down a corridor.

Dev and I moved quickly. We enter in small, windowless room. Bablu was sitting on a metal chair bolted to the floor, his head down, the bright overhead light making him look pale and exhausted.

I pulled out a chair and sat facing him. "The news is everywhere, Bablu. All over the internet, all over TV."

He didn't look up. "I know. I heard the officers talking. Now everything is over for me. My face, my name... it's finished. Just your promise is left." He finally raised his eyes to meet mine. "You promised to protect my brother."

"Yes, I know my promise," I said, leaning forward. "But you see, we are in the same spot now. To protect your brother, to do anything, we have to find Ajay and Sital. You need to try harder, Bablu. Try to recall anything—any small detail you saw or heard that night that could help us. A word, a place name, a face you glimpsed in the car."

"Sir, I swear, I really don't know anything else. I told you everything I know about them already," he said, his voice rising with nervous frustration.

Dev stepped closer, his voice low and serious. "If we find nothing, then the media story becomes the truth. They are already saying you killed Ajay and Sital and threw their bodies in a river. Without another lead, that's the story that will stick. Forever. That's what the world will believe about you."

Bablu's head snapped up, fear flashing in his eyes. "What? Sir, you know that's not true! I didn't kill them!"

"We know that," I said, holding his gaze. "But out there?" I gestured vaguely toward the door, to the world beyond. "Out there, with no other answers, they will believe the worst. You will be remembered not just as a kidnapper, but as a murderer. Your brother will grow up hearing that."

Bablu slumped back, the weight of it crushing him. He closed his eyes tight. He was silent for a long two minutes, the only sound the hum of the air conditioner. Then his eyes flew open.

"What is today's date?" he asked suddenly.

Dev checked his watch. "The 28th."

"The 28th... YES!" Bablu said, a spark of realization lighting his face. "Today is the delivery day! I told you about the timeline before! The Red Meeting was to finalize the shipment, and the delivery is always the next day!"

"Oh!" Dev exclaimed, his own eyes widening. "So yesterday was the Red Meeting... which means today is the delivery to the port!"

A wave of hope surged through me, but it was immediately followed by cold logic. "But there is a problem," I said after a moment, the excitement draining from my voice.

"What, sir?" Dev asked, confused by my sudden shift.

"The news is all over India now. Everyone knows we have Bablu in custody. The traffickers will know their kidnapper has been caught. They will assume he's talking. They'll change their plans. They'll postpone the delivery."

Bablu shook his head. "No, sir, I don't think so. Today is the last day for delivery. The man on the screen—the buyer—he already gave an extension. He was very clear: two weeks, no more. He threatened to go to MASTER JI. He is not a man who accepts delays or excuses. I don't think he will agree to change the plan or give more time just because I got caught. To him, I'm a replaceable tool."

He thought for a second. "All they might do is change the timing of the delivery, or maybe switch to a backup location at the last minute. But the shipment will move today. It has to."

"It's already 4:00 PM," Dev said, checking his watch again. "How do we find them? There are two major ports in Mumbai and dozens of minor ones, fishing villages, private docks..."

"The delivery never happens at the major, busy ports," Bablu interjected. "Too many eyes, too much official activity. It always happens at a small, quiet port or a deserted stretch of coast, so at night, no one notices the movement."

"But there are still so many small ports!" I said, starting to pace the small room. "How do we know which one?"

"Usually, our group used Dharamtar or Trombay for smaller things," Bablu offered. "But because those are known to us, there's a high chance they won't use them this time. They'll assume we might know about them."

"We have to blanket the coastline," I decided, stopping my pacing. "We make teams and send them to every possible port, every landing spot. Dev, go and start organizing. We need every available officer. We have to stop this delivery and, more importantly, we need to grab someone from their team—the driver, a guard, the coordinator—someone who might have heard something about Ajay and Sital. They are our new lead."

"Yes, sir!" Dev said, and hurried out of the room.

I turned to leave, but Bablu's voice stopped me. It was small, filled with dread. "Sir... my brother. Please, protect him. I have a very bad feeling that something will go wrong today."

I walked back and placed a hand on his shoulder. "Nothing is going to happen to him, Bablu. We will find them, at any cost. And yes, I will make sure your brother is safe. You have my word."

I found Dev in the operations room, already pulling up maps on a large screen. We worked quickly, dividing the Mumbai coastline into sectors. We called in officers from nearby stations, pulling in every favor we had. Soon, the room was filled with over fifty officers, all looking tense and determined.

"Everyone, sit down," I called out, and the room quieted. "We have credible information that a major human trafficking shipment is scheduled for delivery tonight at one of the smaller ports along our coast. Our objectives are two-fold: first, intercept that shipment and rescue the victims. Second, and equally critical, we need to capture members of the trafficking team alive for interrogation. They may have information on other missing persons, including our primary case, Ajay and Sital."

I pointed to the map on the screen. "We will work in teams of five. You will wear plain clothes—no uniforms. We cannot spook them. Blend in as fishermen, laborers, or late workers. If you find anything suspicious, you do not engage alone. You inform me or Sub-Inspector Dev immediately. Is that clear?"

A chorus of "Yes, sir!" echoed in the room.

"Focus on the smaller, quieter ports and inlets," Dev added. "The big commercial ports like JNPT are too busy and well-patrolled. They'll avoid them."

"Any questions or suggestions?" I asked.

A seasoned constable raised his hand. "Sir, what if they think exactly that? What if they assume we'll ignore the big ports and then use one precisely because it's busy? They could hide in plain sight."

Dev and I exchanged a look. He was right. "Good point," I said. "We cannot take that risk. We'll have to cover the major ports as well, but with smaller, more discreet teams. It stretches us thin, but we have no choice."

Another officer stood up. "Sir, there is one port, very small, in the far south. It's almost abandoned after sunset. But I've heard rumors... whispers of boats coming and going at odd hours. It's not on most maps. The chances of delivery happening there might be high."

"Good. Note down every location like that—every rumor, every forgotten dock. We check them all," I said. We finalized the team assignments, each group getting a list of ports to cover.

As the teams began to move out, I felt the need to say one more thing. "Listen!" I raised my voice. "We have to find them tonight. The whole city is watching us. The media thinks we are failing. The families are desperate. We have to show Mumbai what its police can do when someone tries to steal our people from us. We fight for them tonight. Jai Ganesh! Jai Siddhivinayak!"

A powerful energy filled the room. Dev stood beside me and shouted, "Bharat Mata Ki—"

"—JAI!" the entire room roared back, the sound vibrating with resolve. I saw it in their eyes—not just duty, but a fierce determination. They filed out, a wave of silent purpose.

"Let's go, Dev," I said. We were assigned to cover the massive Jawaharlal Nehru Port area ourselves, along with a team of three other plainclothes officers. I silenced my phone. Nothing could distract us now.

The drive took forty minutes. As we approached, the scale of the place was daunting—cranes like metal giants, stacks of containers forming canyons, and the endless water with small and big ships on it.

"Start gathering information," I told my team. "Talk to dockworkers, security guards, chai wallahs. Listen for anything unusual—talk of extra night activity, closed-off areas, private security. Move out."

They nodded and melted into the bustling portside environment, which was still active with the day's shift ending. Dev and I walked different side. I go where smaller fishing boats tied to a rickety dock. The smell of salt, fish, and diesel was thick in the air.

"Hello, sir! You want fresh fish?" a small voice said. I looked down. A young girl, no more than ten, stood holding a basket with four sad-looking fish. Her clothes were ragged, her face smudged with dirt.

"No, thank you," I said gently, starting to move past.

"Only one, sir, please," she pleaded, her eyes huge. "I have eaten nothing since morning."

Her words stopped me cold. I looked at her innocent, hungry face. I pulled out a 200-rupee note and handed it to her. “Here. Go eat something good. Something hot.”

She took the note, her eyes wide. “Thank you, sir! But... the man I get the fish from, he takes all our money and only gives us bread to eat.”

Anger stirred in me. “Where is he? I’ll teach him a lesson.”

A spark of hope lit her face. “Yes, sir! I wish someone would. See, he only gave me four fish to sell today. Usually, I get more.”

“Why only four today?” I asked, my detective mind activated.

She shrugged. “Don’t know. Since morning, he has not been behaving well. He is angry and shouting.”

My senses went on alert. Since morning. The day of the shipment. “Where is he now?”

“There,” she said, pointing to a medium-sized, weathered fishing boat about fifty yards down the dock.

A bad feeling settled in my gut. I think he knows something. Or he’s involved.

I walked towards the boat. Two men were standing on the deck, talking in hushed. I moved quietly closer.

“Hey, what do we do now?” one man asked the other.

“Don’t know... Let’s just wait and follow the orders,” the second replied, sounding nervous.

“What’s going on here?” I asked, stepping into view and breaking their conversation.

They both jumped. “Who are you?” the first one demanded.

“What were you two talking about?” I asked, ignoring his question.

"Why should we tell you?" the second one said, puffing out his chest. He took a step closer, then his eyes dropped to the slight bulge under my shirt where my pistol. He step back "Are... are you police?"

"Is that important?" I said, letting my jacket fall open a little more.

"Oh, sorry, sir!" he backtracked, all defiance gone.

"One last time. What were you talking about?"

The first man, now sweating, mumbled, "Sir, there are orders. No fishing from this dock today."

"What? Who gave those orders?"

"Our boss. The owner of this boat."

"Why did he give such orders?"

"We don't know, sir! We were just talking about that! Can we go?"

I studied their frightened faces. They seemed like low-level lackeys, not masterminds. "Yes, you can go. And one more thing—that little girl who sells your fish. You give her proper food, you understand? If I find out you're making children work and starving them, I will come back for you. It will be very bad for you."

They nodded vigorously, muttering "Sorry, sir" again before going.

No fishing today. A specific order. Why? The answer was obvious: to clear the area. To ensure no random fishermen were out on the water to witness something they shouldn't.

Dev found me a few minutes later. "Found anything?"

"Maybe. A couple of dockhands said they have orders for no fishing today. Their boss is on edge."

Dev's eyes narrowed. "I asked around too. A shopkeeper said the same thing. No night fishing crews are going out from this section. I checked with two of our other officers by radio. They're hearing similar things at their assigned docks "

"So the activity is centered here, or at least in this general area," I said, looking out at the forest of shipping containers. "But what do we do with this information? We can't search every container in this port."

"Nothing," Dev said grimly. "We just have to wait and watch. Stay alert."

We spent the next two hours patrolling different sections of the vast port, our eyes straining in the growing darkness. My watch showed 8 PM. Frustration was beginning to set in. Had we guessed wrong? Had they used a different port after all?

Then, I checked my phone. A missed call from one of my constables, just two minutes ago. I immediately called him back.

He picked up on the first ring, his voice a tense whisper. "Sir... come fast. I think we found them."

"What? Where are you? How can you be sure?"

"I'm at the old Warehousing Dock, south sector. There are three big buses and four black cars. They just arrived and are loading buses onto a large cargo ship. It's happening right now!"

"Send me your location! Now!" I ordered.

"I already sent it on the secure messenger app, sir! Check your phone!" The line went dead.

I fumbled with my phone, opening the app. There it was—a pulsing dot on a map about five kilometers away, at a different, more isolated dock within the larger port complex.

"What happened?" Dev asked.

"Constable Patil. He's found them. Three buses, four cars, loading onto a ship. He sent the location. Let's go!"

We ran for our jeep, shouting into our radios for our other three team members to regroup and follow us. This was it. We start, following the GPS.

We had driven about five hundred meters

"Stop the car," I said suddenly.

Dev hit the brakes. "What is it, sir?"

I stared ahead, my mind racing, pieces clicking into place. Then, slowly, I smiled. It was a hard, grim smile. "What do they think we are? Fools?"

Dev looked at me, completely confused. "What?"

"Think, Dev. The same thing happened to us in Dehradun. They are trying to fool us one more time."

Understanding dawned on his face. "The fake tip... the decoy..."

"Exactly," I said, the plan becoming clear. "When that little girl came to me, she was shaking. Nervous. And she had four fish. But today was a 'no fishing' day. Where did those fish come from? They looked fresh. She was planted. And that giant container ship Patil is reporting from? It's been berthed at that old dock for a week according to the port log I skimmed. They want us to rush there. They want all our attention drawn to a dramatic scene on the other side of the port, leaving this area completely empty so they can do their real work quietly, right here."

"You're brilliant, sir," Dev said, a matching grin spreading across his face. He executed a quick U-turn.

"Drive slow. Don't draw attention. Call the others and tell them to converge back on our original position, but to stay hidden. Tell Patil to observe but do NOT engage. It's a trap. We'll need everyone here."

We parked our jeep in a shadowy alley between two warehouses, a good distance from the active docks. We moved the rest of the way on foot, sticking to the deep shadows cast by the towering stacks of shipping containers. The air was cold and smelled of rust and salt.

We found a good vantage point behind a stack of containers and waited, our breaths forming small clouds in the chill. For ten minutes, nothing. Then, we saw movement.

A man emerged from a small guard shack near a gated entrance to a restricted container yard. He looked left and right, pulled out a phone, and made a call. He spoke briefly, then hung up and waited, constantly scanning the area.

About ten minutes later, we heard the low rumble of a heavy engine. A large truck, the kind used to move shipping containers, appeared on the access road, followed by a black sedan. The man at the gate hurried to open it, waving them through.

"This is it," I whispered to Dev.

The truck and sedan drove into the container yard and stopped in a clear area. We moved silently, using the container stacks as cover, getting as close as we dared. We crouched behind a container marked with fading Korean letters.

The driver of the sedan got out. He was a tall, thin man in a dark coat. He pulled out his phone, made another call, speaking quickly.

Minutes later, two black Land Rover Defenders rolled silently into the yard. A man wearing a black ski mask got out of the lead vehicle. He walked up to the tall man, and they shook hands briefly—a business transaction. The masked man then pointed towards the back of the truck.

The tall man barked an order. One of his men, who had been riding in the truck's passenger seat, jumped down and went to the rear. With a loud clang and the hiss of hydraulics, he began unlocking and lowering the heavy rear door of the container.

This was the moment. My grip tightened on my pistol. Inside, I could see shapes huddled together in the dark interior.Men and women, their faces pale with fear in the dim light spilling from the yard lamps. The masked man took a step forward, peered inside, and gave a thumbs-up to the tall man.

"How long for backup to get here?" I whispered to Dev.

"five minutes, maybe ten."

"They're starting to move the people. I'm not waiting. I'll confront them. You and the others, when you hear me, secure the truck and the drivers. Don't let that container door close."

Dev nodded, his face set.

I took a deep breath, stepped out from behind the container, and leveled my pistol. "HANDS UP! ALL OF YOU! POLICE!"

Chaos erupted.

The men around the truck froze for a split second, then scrambled. Weapons were drawn from coats and waistbands. The tall man shouted something and gestured frantically toward the container. The door began to close.

"It will be safer if you put your weapons down and cooperate!" I shouted, advancing.

A gunshot rang out, cracking the night air. Then another. They weren't surrendering.

"OPEN FIRE!" I yelled, diving behind a steel cargo box as bullets sparked off the metal around me. The sharp, deafening reports of pistols and the deeper thump of a submachine gun filled the yard.

From my small vision, I saw Dev and two other officers, who had just arrived, fan out, returning fire and moving tactically toward the truck. Their focus was on the tall man and his guards, who were using the truck and sedan for cover.

My eyes locked on the masked man. While his guards engaged us, he was bent low, scurrying like a rat back toward his black Defender. He's the boss. We need him alive.

I broke from my cover, using the chaos and the maze of containers as a shield. I ran in a wide arc, coming up behind the row of containers where the Defender was parked. As I rounded the last corner, I came face-to-face with him. He was fumbling with the car door handle.

I raised my gun. "FREEZE! HANDS UP!"

He stiffened, his shoulders slumping in defeat. Slowly, he raised his hands.

"Turn around. Slowly. Now take off the mask."

He turned. His hands, trembling, went to his head. He pulled off the ski mask.

I was staring at a man in his forties with pale white skin, sharp features, and neatly combed golden hair. He didn't look like a local thug. He looked... foreign. European, perhaps.

"Please," he said, his accent thick, Eastern European. "Leave me. I can pay."

Before I could respond, a tremendous force slammed into my side. I was thrown to the hard concrete, the breath knocked out of me. My pistol skittered away into the darkness. A hulking man—one of the tall man's guards—stood over me, having blindsided me from another container row.

The golden-haired man didn't hesitate. He yanked his mask back on, wrenched open the car door, and jumped into the driver's seat. The engine roared to life.

"NO!" I shouted, scrambling to my feet. The guard who had tackled me charged again. I sidestepped his punch and drove my fist into his face. He grunted and doubled over. I followed with a hard uppercut to his jaw. He crumpled to the ground, unconscious.

But it was too late. The black Defender's tires screeched, spraying gravel, as it shot out of the container yard and vanished into the night.

"SHIT!" I screamed in frustration. I retrieved my gun and ran back toward the main firefight.

The scene was stabilizing. The tall man were pinned down behind the sedan, which was now riddled with bullet holes. Dev was providing covering fire from behind a forklift.

I caught Dev's eye and signaled I was going to flank them from the other side. He nodded, increasing his rate of fire to draw their attention.

I moved silently along the back of the containers, coming up behind the sedan. I could hear the tall man panting, yelling into a phone. "We are under attack! We need—"

I lunged, grabbing him in a chokehold from behind, yanking him away from the car. I disarmed him with a sharp twist of his wrist and shoved him to the ground, placing my knee on his back and my gun to his head. "SURRENDER!" I bellowed at the remaining two guards.

Seeing their leader captured, their fight left them. They dropped their weapons and raised their hands.

At that moment, the beautiful sound of multiple police sirens wailed, growing louder. Reinforcements poured into the yard, securing the remaining criminals and fanning out to secure the area.

An officer took the tall man from me, cuffing him roughly. I stood up, my chest heaving. Dev jogged over to me.

"All good, sir?" he asked.

"Yes. But the main one, the foreigner, got away in his car," I said, the failure bitter in my mouth.

Dev nodded, disappointed, but then gestured to the truck. "But we stopped the shipment."

I looked at the massive container, its door still half-open. A wave of profound relief and satisfaction washed over the bitterness. We had done it. "We saved a lot of lives tonight, Dev."

"Yes, sir," he said, a genuine smile breaking through.

We walked together toward the container. The victims inside had to be terrified. We needed to reassure them, get them medical attention.

"Open it fully," I told an officer with a flashlight. He cranked the door the rest of the way up, and a bright beam pierced the dark interior.

I stepped forward, a reassuring smile on my face. "Don't be scared! It's over! We are the police! You are all safe now! You can come out!"

But nobody moved. No sounds of relief, no scrambling to freedom. They just sat there, huddled, their faces shadowed.

"What's wrong?" I murmured, taking a step closer, peering into the gloom.

Then, everything happened in slow motion.

One of the figures near the front stood up. But not with the weak, grateful posture of a victim. He stood up with purpose. The beam of the flashlight caught the glint of metal in his hand.

It wasn't a victim. It was a guard who had hidden among them.

My expression changed from relief to horror in an instant.

The world went silent. I saw the muzzle flash.

But my eyes were on Dev.

I saw his body jolt. I saw a dark, wet patch instantly bloom and spread across the center of his chest, stark against his light shirt. His smile vanished, replaced by a look of pure shock. His eyes met mine, wide and confused.

"SIR!!" he shouted, but his voice was already weak, choked.

Then his legs buckled. He fell to his knees, and then crumpled forward onto the ground.

"DEV!" My own scream tore from my throat. my training and rage took over. I raised my pistol, my vision tunneling on the man in the container. I fired. Once. Twice. Three times. The shots were deafening in the confined space. The man jerked and fell back, disappearing into the darkness.

Other officers rushed forward, guns drawn, shouting.

But I didn't see them. I stumbled to where Dev lay. I dropped to my knees beside him, my hands going to the horrific wound on his chest. Blood was everywhere, hot and slick, pumping out with every faint beat of his heart.

"Dev... Dev, listen to me! Open your eyes, Dev! LOOK AT ME!" I shouted, my voice cracking. I pressed my hands hard against the wound, trying to stem the impossible flow. "SOMEONE CALL AN AMBULANCE! NOW! MOVE! NOW!"

CHAPTER TWENTY

HOPE

We lifted Dev into the back of a police jeep as gently as we could, but every jolt of the vehicle on the rough road made him groan in pain. He was breathing, but it was shallow and ragged, each inhale a desperate. The dark stain on his chest seemed to grow with every passing second. I kept my hands pressed hard against the wound, my own shirt soaked with his blood, shouting at the driver to go faster while trying to keep Dev conscious.

"Stay with me, Dev. Look at me. Don't close your eyes," I kept repeating, my voice trembling. His eyes were half-closed, glazed with shock. Fifteen minutes felt like an hour.

We finally screeched to a halt outside the emergency entrance of the nearest major hospital. I leapt out, screaming for help. "We need a stretcher! Now!"

Medical staff came rushing out. A doctor in green scrubs took one look at Dev and his expression turned grim. "What happened?"

"Gunshot wound to the chest," I said, my words clipped.

"Get him to emergency Room One, now!" the doctor ordered. I jogged beside them as they wheeled him through the sliding doors, down a bright, corridor. At the doors to the operating theater, a nurse stopped me.

"You have to wait here, sir."

I was left standing alone in the hallway, the doors swinging shut with a final, heavy sound. My hands were sticky and red. I leaned against the cold wall, my legs weak. I slid down to the floor, my head in my hands. I couldn't pray, I couldn't think. All I could see was Dev falling, the look of surprise on his face.

A young constable who had followed us in hesitantly approached. "Inspector Sir... Dev Sir will be fine. He's strong."

I just nodded, unable to speak. My mind replayed the scene over and over. It was my plan. My order to rush in.

Thirty minutes later, the surgeon emerged. His face was lined with fatigue and something else—concern. My heart felt like it stopped beating.

"Doctor? What's happening?" I asked, scrambling to my feet.

"We are trying our best, but..." he began, choosing his words carefully. "The bullet is lodged in a very sensitive area, near the lung and close to a major blood vessel. It entered at an angle that makes it extremely difficult to remove without causing more damage. Do you understand what I am saying?"

I shook my head, not wanting to understand. "No! What are you saying? Just tell me you can save him. That's all I need to hear!"

The doctor's face softened with pity. "You need to call his family. He needs them here. As for his chances... I would say it is 60-40."

"What does that mean? 60-40? Tell me in plain language, please," I demanded, my voice cracking.

"There is a 60 percent chance he may not survive the surgery or the complications. A 40 percent chance he pulls through. I'm sorry. We are doing everything we can. A specialist thoracic surgeon is on his way. Until then, we are stabilizing him." Without another word, he turned and went back through the doors.

Sixty percent. The numbers echoed in the silent hallway. Dying.

"No... no, no, no..." I whispered, slumping back against the wall.

I turned to the constable. "Call his family. Get them here. Now."

Another half-hour crawled by. Each second was a torture. Then, a tall, older doctor in a long white coat arrived, spoke briefly to a nurse, and disappeared into the OR. The specialist. A few minutes after that, Dev's mother and younger sister arrived. They were both weeping, their faces pale with terror.

"Where is my son? Where is Dev?" his mother cried, clutching her daughter's arm for support.

I moved toward them, trying to project a calm I didn't feel. "He's in surgery, ma'am. The best doctors are with him. You have to believe in him. He's a fighter."

She looked at me, her eyes searching my face. "You are... Veer?"

"Yes, ma'am."

Tears streamed down her face. "He always says on the phone, 'I'm working with Veer Bhaiya. He takes care of me like a brother. I am so happy working with him.'" She reached out and held both my hands in hers. Her trust was a knife in my gut.

I bowed my head, the guilt overwhelming me. "I am so sorry, ma'am. It was my plan... my decision to rush in..."

A sob escaped me. I couldn't hold back the tears any longer. I had led my friend, her son, into that ambush.

Another hour passed. The clock on the wall ticked continusly. His sister paced. His mother sat silently, lips moving in silent prayer.

What is taking so long? If he dies... I will never forgive myself. Never.

Finally, the doors opened again. The specialist emerged, removing his surgical cap. We all rushed forward.

"Doctor?" His mother's voice was a thin thread of hope.

The doctor's stern face broke into a small, tired smile. "He is out of immediate danger. He's a very lucky young man."

The relief that washed over me was so profound my knees almost buckled. It was like a crushing weight had been lifted from my chest, allowing me to breathe for the first time in hours.

"How is he? Will he be completely fine?" Dev's sister asked, crying with relief.

"He will need complete rest for at least a week, maybe more. No work, no stress. The next 24 hours are critical for monitoring, but the worst is over. You can see him briefly in the morning; he's sedated now and needs to sleep."

"Thank you, Doctor. Thank you so much," I said, shaking his hand.

"It's 1:00 AM," Dev's mother said, turning to me. Her face was etched with exhaustion, but concern for me was now in her eyes. "You look terrible. You need to rest."

My eyes burned with fatigue, and a deep, bone-aching tiredness had settled in. "I want to, ma'am, but we captured a man tonight. I have to interrogate him. He might know something."

I took a step, and my leg trembled violently. I had to grab the wall for support. I had been running on adrenaline and fear for two straight days without a moment of real rest. My body was shutting down.

The constable was at my side instantly. "Sir, she is right. You are in no state to interrogate anyone. We have the man secure at headquarters. Let me take you home. You can talk to him with a clear head in the morning."

He was right. In my current state, I'd be useless. I'd miss clues, lose my temper. "Okay. Take me home."

He drove me to my home. The world outside the car window was a blur. "Take care, sir," he said as I got out.

I fumbled with my keys, entered my dark, silent home, and peeled off my blood-stained clothes. I didn't have the energy to eat or even shower properly. I fell onto my bed and was swallowed by a deep, dreamless sleep almost before my head hit the pillow.

The next morning marked the tenth day since Ajay and Sital had disappeared.

I woke up feeling disoriented but physically better. The sleep had been a reset. I took a long, hot shower, letting the water wash away the grime and some of the lingering horror. When I came out, Priya, my housekeeper, had laid out breakfast.

"Here is your breakfast, sir," she said softly, placing a plate of poha and tea in front of me.

I ate ravenously. I hadn't realized how starved I was. Every bite tasted like life itself. As I ate, I checked my phone. The screen was a chaos of notifications: dozens of missed calls and messages.

My mother—15 missed calls. A pang of guilt hit me. I called her back immediately.

"Veer! Are you alright?" she answered on the third ring, her voice tight with panic.

"Yes, Mom. I'm fine. Don't worry."

"Don't worry? The news is everywhere! All the relatives are calling about 'your case.' Your interview, the shooting at the port... and you didn't pick up your phone a single time! Do you know I haven't slept?" Her fear had turned to anger, which was her way of caring.

"I'm so sorry, Mom. My phone was on silent. Everything happened so fast..."

"And Dev? Is he alright?" The anger faded, replaced by maternal concern.

"He's out of danger now," I said, the relief still fresh.

"Thank God," she breathed. "Okay. But be safe. Call me."

"I will, Mom. I promise."

I scrolled through the other messages—from colleagues, superiors, unknown numbers—and ignored them all. My focus had to be absolute.

I have to talk to that tall man from the port.

It took forty minutes to drive to headquarters. The station was buzzing with an unusual energy. As I walked in, a senior constable approached me, looking uneasy.

"Sir, I need to tell you something," he said in a low voice.

"What is it?"

"Sir, that man we caught last night... the tall one. He has confessed. He says he is guilty of kidnapping Ajay and Sital. He says he killed them both and dumped their bodies in a jungle."

The words didn't make sense. They bounced off my brain. "What? How... that's not possible."

"It's true, sir. He gave a full statement. The case... it's solved."

Solved. The word was like a foreign object. My mind rejected it completely. This is a lie. A setup.

"Where is he? I want to talk to him myself."

"Interrogation Room Three, sir."

I marched down the hallway, my confusion hardening into determination. I threw open the door to the small room. The man was there, sitting calmly, his eyes closed as if in meditation.

"Wake up," I snarled, slamming my palm on the metal table. The sound echoed in the small room.

He opened his eyes slowly, a smug look on his face. "What is it? I already told you everything. I accept it. I killed them both."

"No, you're lying," I said, leaning over the table. "I know you didn't do it. They are alive."

"I did," he stated flatly.

"Was it MASTER JI? Did he order you to say this?" I pressed.

A flicker of surprise crossed his face, then it was gone. "Oh, so Bablu told you about MASTER JI? I knew he wasn't strong enough. But it doesn't matter. I killed them. I take responsibility for all the kidnappings. The case is closed." He gave me a thin, cold smile.

"Where did you dump the bodies, then?" I asked, testing him.

"I don't know the exact place. It was very dark."

"Why did you kill them?"

"I hated them. They were rich. I was going to ask for money, but they woke up and tried to run. So I used my knife. Simple."

His story was generic, devoid of the specific, chilling details that usually accompany a true confession. It was a script.

"I know you didn't do it," I said firmly, turning to leave.

As my hand touched the doorknob, he spoke again, his voice dropping to a menacing whisper. "You can't win a fight against MASTER JI. And after you messed up our delivery, he will be very upset. He will do something to you... something you can't even imagine." He started to laugh, a dry, hollow sound.

I walked out, the laugh echoing in my ears. In the corridor, I almost collided with IG sir. He was beaming.

"Veer! My boy! You solved it!" He clapped me on the shoulder and pulled me into a brief, hearty hug.

"Sir, he's not the killer. He's lying," I said, pulling back.

The IG's smile vanished. "What? Stop this now, Veer."

"No, sir. Both of them are alive. Someone else is behind this. You have to believe me."

His face hardened. "The case is closed, Veer. We have a confession. We will announce it to the media. The court hearing is day after tomorrow. I don't want any more complications. Do you understand?"

"I want to give real justice to their families, sir," I pleaded.

"You have. By catching this man. Now, let the process work." His tone was final. He gave me a last, warning look and walked away.

I stood there, feeling the walls close in. I got in my car to drive to the hospital to see Dev, my mind racing.

(No, Veer. This can't be true and you know it. What about the woman Bablu mentioned? The five-lakh advance payment just for a kidnapping? The plane tickets to Dehradun? The promotion to Group C? All that for a simple murder they could have arranged locally? No. This is a cover-up. MASTER JI is sacrificing this pawn to protect the bigger operation and to bury the truth about Ajay and Sital forever.)

I reached the hospital and found Dev's room. His mother and sister were just leaving.

"He's awake, Inspector," his mother said. "We're just going home to get some clothes and things."

I entered the room. Dev was propped up on pillows, looking pale and tired but very much alive. A monitor beeped steadily beside him.

"Hello, Dev. How are you feeling?" I asked, pulling up a chair.

He opened his eyes and tried to sit up. "Sir..."

"Easy, relax," I said, gently pressing him back.

"When the bullet hit me... I saw my father. He was standing there, trying to help me. Then I saw my mother and sister waiting for me to come home." His voice was weak but clear.

"You're home now, Dev. You're safe."

After a moment of silence, he asked, "What about the man from the port?"

I sighed. "He's taken full responsibility. He says he kidnapped and killed Ajay and Sital."

Dev's eyes widened. "What? But... Bablu said they were important. Special. Why would they go through all that trouble just to kill them? It doesn't make sense."

"It doesn't. But the IG wants the case closed. Quickly."

"What do we do now, sir?"

"I don't know, Dev. The hearing is day after tomorrow. Once a verdict is given based on this false confession, the search for them will officially end. MASTER JI will have won."

My phone rang. It was Ruhi. I answered.

"Veer! Are you okay? You haven't been picking up! Your mother told me you were fine, but with everything on the news..." Her voice was a mix of worry and frustration.

"I'm okay, Ruhi. Really."

"Listen, I have to tell you something. I'm taking the case."

"What case?"

"The prosecution. For the tall man. I've been assigned as the public prosecutor."

A spark of hope. "That's good. But Ruhi... the case is 'solved.' He confessed."

"I know. But the judge still has to sentence him. And there's news that a top, expensive lawyer has been hired to defend him. They'll try to get his sentence reduced, maybe even argue he was coerced. I won't let someone who did this walk easy. I'm going for the maximum."

"Ruhi, I need to tell you something," I said, lowering my voice. "He didn't kill Ajay and Sital."

There was a stunned silence on the other end. "What are you talking about, Veer?"

"I can't prove it yet. But I know it. I have one day to find something, anything."

"Veer, if you have a theory, you need evidence! Solid proof! Or no one will listen, not even me in a courtroom!"

"I'll find it," I said, more to convince myself than her. "I have to." I ended the call.

"I have to go, Dev. I have one day."

"I'll help, sir. I can make calls from here," he said, already reaching for his phone on the bedside table.

"No. Your only job is to rest and get better. That's an order." I managed a weak smile and left.

I drove back to headquarters, a plan forming. I needed to question the tall man again, push him on the inconsistencies. But as I walked down the familiar corridor, a man in an expensive suit stepped into my path. He was a lawyer I recognized—one of the city's most ruthless defense attorneys.

"Inspector veer," he said smoothly. "The investigation phase is over. My client has confessed. No further interrogations are permitted without my presence, and I am denying all requests. If you attempt to enter that room, I will file for harassment and have your involvement in this case reviewed."

I stared at him, my anger boiling. This was MASTER JI's hand, moving pieces on a board. "I am going in," I said, trying to step around him.

He didn't move. "I'd advise against it, Inspector. The order comes from higher up than you. Try it, and we will take official action against you."

The threat was clear. I was locked out. I turned on my heel and walked back to my car, slamming the door shut. I just sat there, hands gripping the steering wheel until my knuckles were white.

This is not good. What is happening? If this goes through, we will never find them. Think, Veer. THINK.

Hours passed. I drove around aimlessly, my mind a frantic blank. I checked the news on my phone. Headlines celebrated the "Swift Police Work" and "Case Cracked in Dramatic Shootout." The public was relieved. The pressure on the department was easing. Everyone was happy to have a monster in a cage.

Everyone but me, and two families who would never have closure, and two kids who were still out there somewhere.

I closed my eyes, leaning my head against the car window. A feeling of utter helplessness washed over me. God, or whoever is listening... help me give them justice. Everyone is against me. I'm stuck. There's not a single clue left.

As if in direct answer, my phone rang. An unknown number. A faint, desperate hope flickered.

"Hello?"

"Inspector? This is Sital's father." His voice was quiet, strained.

My heart leapt into my throat. "Yes, sir. What is it?"

"Can we meet? At your police station? There is something... my daughter wants to tell you. She remembers something."

"Of course. I'll be there in twenty minutes." I ended the call, my mind already racing. Could it be? After all this?

I drove to the station, every possibility flying through my mind. Was it a detail about her kidnapping? A face? A sound?

I entered and saw them in the waiting area: Sital's father, looking older and wearier than I remembered, and beside him, the young girl. Her sister

My initial hope faltered. "Please, come to my office."

Once inside, Sital's father spoke. "Inspector, my daughter told me something last night. She made me promise to tell you. She insisted you should hear it directly from her."

I turned to the girl, who looked nervous, clutching her father's arm. "Yes, beta? What did you see?" I asked, as gently as I could.

"I... I saw something," she began, her voice barely a whisper.

"What?" The word came out louder than I intended, driven by sudden, fierce hope. She flinched, scared.

I took a deep breath, calming myself. "I'm sorry, beta. I didn't mean to shout. Please, take your time. Tell me what you saw."

And she began to talk. Slowly, haltingly, she told her story. It wasn't about the night of the kidnapping. It was about 1 month before. As she spoke, the pieces began to fall into place, not with a gentle click, but with the force of the truth.

Then she said something that made the earth seem to drop from under my feet

I sat in stunned silence, the air sucked from the room. If what she said was true... then Ajay and Sital were not dead. They were being held somewhere.

"Are you absolutely sure about what you heard?" I asked her, my voice trembling.

"Yes, sir," she said, more confidently now. "I remember because I thought, 'Ajay bhaiya? Like the missing boy on TV?' But I was too scared to say anything."

I turned to her father. "Sir, you mentioned sleeping pills earlier. What about them?"

"Yes, Inspector. My daughter... Sital... she sometimes had terrible trouble sleeping during exams. Our family doctor prescribed mild sleeping pills for her".

"If this is true... then the whole case just changed," I whispered. "Now I have to recheck everything."

I thanked the girl and her father, promised to keep her safe, and started gathering other information the tall man name is 'VIKRAM SOLANKI' and quietly to double-check my new doubt. Talked to neighbors, rechecked old statements, timings, alibis—everything. It take me whole next day but Piece by piece, a new picture emerged. It wasn't complete, but it was enough to shatter the official story.

December 30st. The day of the court hearing. [TENTH day since missing]

I rushed to the courthouse, a thick file clutched under my arm. Outside, I saw Ruhi, looking professional and formidable in her lawyer's gown, reviewing notes.

"Ruhi! I need to talk to you!" I called out, hurrying over.

"Veer! Where have you been? You said they were alive. What is going on?" she asked, her confusion battling with her professional composure.

"Not here. Somewhere private." We found a quiet alcove away from the gathering crowd of media and onlookers.

"Now, tell me. What did you find?"

"I solved the case," I said, a genuine smile breaking through my exhaustion.

Her eyes widened. "You found the real person behind it?"

"Yes. And I have proof. Not all of it, but enough to blow a hole in their confession."

"Tell me now. And it better be solid, Veer. Without proof, it's just a story."

I handed her the file. "It's all in here. Witness statement from the sital little sister, phone record analysis showing a call to a private medical service, property records. But you need to be ready for a shock."

I starts telling her about everything that I found and When I finished, Ruhi's hand flew to her mouth. She stared at me,

"Veer... Do you know what you're saying? This changes everything. It means the entire prosecution is based on a lie. It means the real victims are still out there!"

"I know. Now, take this file and give their families real justice."

Ten minutes later, a police van arrived. Bablu and Vikram Solanki were led inside in handcuffs, surrounded by a media frenzy. The hearing began. The courtroom was packed: the families of the missing, Anil and his mother with sonam, and important public.

The judge, an elderly man with a stern face, opened the proceedings. "This case appears to be straightforward. The accused has confessed to the kidnappings and murders. We are here for sentencing arguments."

Ruhi stood up, her voice clear and confident. "My Lord, the case is not over. There is significant reason to believe that the Ajay and Sital, are still alive."

The courtroom erupted. Gasps, shouts, the frantic scratching of pens. Vikram's high-priced defense lawyer looked momentarily stunned. The judge banged his gavel. "Order! Order! Silence!"

He glared at Ruhi. "What are you saying? The accused has confessed!"

"Yes, My Lord. But I have new evidence that casts serious doubt on that confession and indicates a conspiracy to obstruct justice. I request permission to call a witness to the stand."

"What witness? This is highly irregular!"

"A witness whose testimony directly contradicts the accused's story and provides a lead on the victims' whereabouts."

The judge frowned, intrigued despite himself. "Who is this witness?"

Ruhi took a deep breath, her eyes meeting mine across the room. I gave her a slight, encouraging nod.

"My Lord, I call to the stand... SONAM."

A fresh wave of confusion and murmuring swept the room. Everyone looked around. From the back of the courtroom, a young woman stood up. It was Sital's best friend, the one we had spoken to on the first day.

All eyes were on her. All eyes except mine. Mine were fixed on Vikram Solanki in the dock. For the first time, I saw a crack in his arrogant facade. A flicker of pure, undiluted fear.

CHAPTER TWENTY-ONE

THE TRUTH

"What?" Sonam stammered from the public stand, her expression shifting from confusion to panic.

The courtroom erupted once again, louder and more aggressively than before. Reporters whispered frantically into their phones, the families of the missing gasped, and Vikram Solanki's lawyer leaned over to confer with his client in urgent, hushed tones.

"Order! Order! Please keep the decorum of the court!" the judge bellowed, banging his gavel. When the noise subsided to a low, excited hum, he fixed Ruhi with a piercing stare. "You are claiming that this man, who has confessed to murder, is not guilty?"

"No, My Lord," Ruhi replied, her voice crisp and confident. "I am not claiming he is innocent of all crimes. The evidence shows he is guilty of human trafficking. But I am stating, and I have proof, that he is not the murderer of Ajay and Sital. I believe they are still alive."

A fresh wave of murmurs swept the room.

The judge leaned back, intrigued. "We are here for justice. If you have evidence that the victims may be alive, it is my duty to hear it. Permission granted. Ms. Sonam, please step forward to the witness box."

Sonam, looking pale and terrified, walked on unsteady legs to the witness box and was sworn in. She clutched the wooden railing as if it were the only thing holding her up.

Ruhi approached, her heels clicking on the polished floor. "Now, Ms. Sonam, let's start at the beginning. Where were you on the evening of December 18th?"

"At... at my home," Sonam whispered.

"And what happened that evening? Tell the court in your own words."

"I was studying for my pre-board exams. Then, I got a group call from Anil. We talked about Sital, who had sent us a 'help me' message. We tried calling her back, but she didn't pick up. Finally, I remembered it was a prank she had talked about a few days earlier. We decided to meet at school the next day to talk about it. That's all."

"And what happened the next day at school?"

"She said she'd been sleeping and didn't know who had sent the messages."

"So," Ruhi said, turning to address the judge, "according to this, someone allegedly broke into Sital's home, took her phone, unlocked it, sent specific messages to her friends, and then left without a trace. Does that sound normal to you, My Lord?"

Sonam shifted uncomfortably. "I don't know. Anything is possible."

"Don't lie, Sonam," Ruhi said sharply, turning back to her. "Tell the court the truth. You were the one who sent those messages from Sital's account. And we have proof from the social media company showing two active logins for that account that night—one from Sital's phone, and one from yours. Sital was drugged with her own sleeping pills. The police found an almost-full packet in her home, with only two pills missing. The chemist confirmed the prescription was filled just two days prior. She took one the first night, and one the night of the 18th. She was unconscious. She couldn't have sent anything."

Sonam's eyes darted around the room, looking for an escape. "Yes... I sent those messages. But that doesn't prove I kidnapped anyone!"

"Then why did you send them, Sonam? And why did you hide it from the police?" Ruhi pressed, her voice rising.

"For fun! It was a stupid joke! I was scared that if I told the police, I'd get arrested for harassment!"

"Don't lie!" Ruhi's voice cut through the courtroom like a whip. "Your neighbor gave a statement. She said you were home that night, but you were behaving strangely—agitated, not like yourself. We know everything now, Sonam. We know what happened at Sital's house one month ago. Tell the court. Tell us about Anshul."

The name hit Sonam like a physical blow. Her composure shattered. "I... I don't... I didn't do that..." she stammered, tears welling in her eyes.

"Tell us, Sonam! Where are they? They were your friends!" Ruhi moved closer, applying relentless pressure.

"NO! SHE WAS NOT MY FRIEND!" Sonam screamed, the raw outburst silencing the entire courtroom. "She was not my friend! She stole the boy I loved! What would you do if your best friend did that to you? Tell me!"

A cold wave of satisfaction washed over me. I allowed myself a small, grim smile, recalling my conversation with Sital's younger sister just the day before.

('Tell me, beta, what did you want to tell me?' I had asked the little girl.

'One month ago... when Mom was talking to Sital Didi on the phone, she gave the phone to me. I talked a little, then said bye. But the phone wasn't disconnected. I heard

Didi talking to Sonam Didi. They were shouting.'

'How did you know it was Sonam Didi, beta?'

'I know her voice. She always talks to me.'

'What did you hear?'

'They were both shouting. They kept saying one name... An... Ansh... Anshul.'

'Do you know who Anshul is?'

'Yes. He is a very nice bhaiya. He always talks politely to me. But it was a secret. Didi told me not to tell our parents, and I would be the best sister in the world. But now I see Mother crying, and I thought I should tell everything I know.'

'Oh, thank you so much, beta. You are the best sister in the world. Is there anything else?'

'Mmm... yes. One day when we went to Didi's house, Sonam Didi was there. She was asking Sital Didi for her phone ID to talk to someone. I didn't understand properly.'

That conversation had sent me digging into Sonam's life, her relationships, and her recent activities. The picture that emerged was one of envy and simmering rage.)

"Your plan is over, Sonam," Ruhi said, her voice now cold and clinical. "Tell the court properly. What did you do to her?"

Sonam broke down completely. Sobbing, her shoulders shaking, she began to speak.

Sonam's Story:

"It all started about a month and a half ago," she began, her voice a broken monotone. "I went to Sital's flat. 'Hi, Sital,' I said.

'Come in, yaar! Why are you standing outside?' she replied.

'What are you doing? Making grilled sandwiches?'

'Yes. Do you want some?'

I looked at her, and we both laughed. 'You wait in my room. I'll be there with tea and sandwiches.'

I waited in her room, looking at her books. She came in with a plate. I saw a new novel on her bedside table. '"Love Triangle,"' I read aloud. 'I think someone is in love...'

'No, yaar, it's just for reading,' she said, but she blushed.

We talked for the next hour about all sorts of things—college, movies, plans. 'Okay, I should go,' I said, checking my watch. 'I need your physics notes, chapter six.'

'Okay, take them.' She handed me the notes. As I was leaving, I felt thirsty, so I went to the kitchen for a glass of water. That's when I saw it. On the refrigerator door, held by a magnet, was a piece of paper. On it was written a name: 'ANSHUL,' with a little heart drawn next to it.

My blood ran cold. 'What is this, Sital?' I asked, my voice tight.

'Oh, that's nothing...' she stammered, trying to take the paper.

'What are you doing? You know he was my crush! What is this?'

'Sonam, he doesn't like you that way. He told me,' she said softly.

'What? You're a liar!' I was so hurt, so angry. I threw her notes on the floor and ran out of the house.

The next day, I apologized. I didn't want to lose our friendship. But the hurt festered inside me. He was my crush. How could she do this? I started ignoring her, but the bitterness only grew. I decided I had to show her. I had to make her feel small, make her pay for thinking she was prettier, better than me.

The idea started as a dark fantasy, but it took root. I wanted her to suffer. I wanted her to disappear. A friend of mine knew some people from the wrong side of the city. He told me about a guy named Bablu who 'fixed problems' for money. So on the one day in the park

I made the call. My hands were shaking. 'Hello, is this Bablu?'

'Yes, speaking,' a rough voice answered.

'I... I will give you a lot of money. I need you to kidnap a girl for me.'

'How much?'

'Five lakh rupees.'

There was a pause. 'Okay. Send me the date and other details.'

'Tell me your address. I'll send you a parcel with all the information and the advance.' I hung up, my heart pounding.

As I turned from the corner where I'd made the call, I froze. Ajay was standing there. He had heard everything. His face was a mask of horror.

'What are you doing, Sonam? Whose kidnapping?' he asked, his voice trembling.

'No one's! It's nothing!' I said, panicked.

'If you do that to anyone, I will go straight to the police. Do you hear me? You are not doing this!'

'Listen to me, Ajay,' I said, stepping closer, my mind racing.

'Stay away from me!' He pushed me back, his eyes wide with fear and disgust. 'I don't want to hurt you, but you cannot do something like this. You're a human being!'

'I promise, Ajay! I'm sorry, I'm just... I'm just really mad right now,' I pleaded, forcing tears.

'What happened? Tell me. Maybe we can find a solution. Who is it?'

I couldn't tell him it was Sital. So I made up a story about a school rival. He listened, his face softening slightly.

'I'll talk to Shiva. We'll figure out how to handle this guy at school. We already make fun of him by throwing soda cans..You don't have to do these crazy things.' He even gave me a brief, awkward hug before leaving. 'Just promise me you'll drop this.'

I promised. But the moment he was gone, my anger returned, hotter than before. How dare he push me? How dare he judge me?

I checked to make sure he was really gone, then I called Bablu again. 'Bablu, there's a change. Now there are two people.'

'No. That's too risky.'

'I'll give you ten lakh. For both.'

A longer pause. Then, '...Done.'

I gathered photos of both Sital and Ajay. I put them in a box with a note detailing their routines—Ajay leaving his house around 7:50 PM for the MT building, Sital passing by later. I included a five-lakh advance. I sent it to the address Bablu gave me.

The next day at school, Ajay, trying to 'help' me with my fake problem, got into a fight with Shiva. Later, he came to me, a small smile on his face. 'Okay, happy now?' he asked.

I smiled back. But my plan was already in motion.

On the night of December 18th, I took alcohol to calm my nerves. While feeling drowsy, a wicked idea struck. I accessed Sital's social media account—she'd logged in on my phone once and I'd saved the password. I sent those 'help me' messages to the group chat. I thought it would make her look hysterical and stupid later. But then Anil called, and the reality of what I'd done began to scare me.

The next day, December 19th, was the day. I knew Ajay's parents were leaving for an event that evening; he'd told me about it. Before the planned study group, I sent Ajay a message from Sital's account. 'Hey Ajay, I'm stuck at the MT building. Can you come pick me up? Please, it's urgent.'

He replied instantly. 'On my way.' And he left his house.

I had already given Bablu the location and time. My part was done. I went to the meeting spot myself, acting normal, so no one would suspect me later. Anil arrived on his bike. We waited. Of course, Ajay never came. I knew he wouldn't.

Then Sital arrived, looking confused. Seeing her face, hearing her worried voice asking about Ajay, filled me with a dark satisfaction. Her words from a month ago echoed in my ears: 'He doesn't like you that way.'

After some time, Anil got angry, saying he was leaving to get food. I went with him. It was perfect. When the kidnappings were discovered, I could say I was with Anil the whole time.

At the restaurant, I excused myself to the washroom. Inside, I texted Bablu. 'Got him?'

The reply came quickly. 'Yes.'

I took a deep, shuddering breath. Then I texted, 'The girl will be there soon. Be ready.'

I called Sital, putting panic into my voice. 'Sital! We found Ajay! He's at the MT building, and he's hurt! You need to come quickly!'

'What? Oh my god! I'll be there in ten minutes!' she said, and hung up.

A feeling of cold, powerful triumph washed over me. Then I washed my face, changed my expression to one of concern, and went back to the table.

Anil dropped me home afterwards. I waited until his bike was out of sight, then I hailed an autorickshaw and gave the driver the address of the JJ Club. It took forty minutes to get there.

In the dark alley behind the club, I saw a car. I walked closer. Through the window, I saw them. Both Ajay and Sital were in the backseat, unconscious, slumped against each other. Bablu was standing outside, smoking.

He saw me and nodded. 'It's done. The rest of the money?'

'You'll get it when I know they're where they need to be,' I said, my voice surprisingly steady. I looked at my former friends, their peaceful, drugged faces, and felt nothing but cold victory."

Sonam finished her story, collapsing into fresh, heaving sobs.

A profound, horrified silence gripped the courtroom. The judge looked stunned. The families of Ajay and Sital stared at Sonam with a mixture of disbelief and utter hatred. Vikram Solanki simply looked bored, as if this personal drama was beneath him.

But where is MASTER JI in all this? I thought, my mind racing. This is a story of personal revenge, not a grand conspiracy. She's leaving something huge out.

Ruhi broke the silence. "You are not a woman; you are a criminal," she stated coldly. "Now, the most important question. Where are they now?"

Sonam cried harder, her words barely intelligible. "They... they are in my house."

"What?!" I was on my feet instantly. "My Lord, permission to—"

The judge didn't let me finish. "Court is adjourned until the police can confirm the presence of the victims at that location! Officer, proceed!"

I didn't wait for another word. I ran. Two constables sprinted after me. We burst out of the courthouse and into my waiting car.

"Drive! Fast! To Sonam's residence!" I barked at the driver.

We sped through the city, sirens blaring. My mind was a whirlwind. Alive. They might be alive.

Twenty-five minutes later, we screeched to a halt outside a modest, standalone house painted a fading white. It looked utterly ordinary, peaceful.

"Break the gate!" I ordered.

The constables used a battering ram from the car trunk. The lock gave way with a sharp crack. We rushed inside. The house was neat, quiet. Too quiet.

"Search every room! Check for a basement, an attic, a locked room!"

I moved through the living room, my eyes scanning for anything out of place. Then I saw it—a door in the hallway, different from the others. It was heavy, with a new, sturdy lock. A basement door.

"Here! Break this!"

One of the constables raised the ram and slammed it into the door near the lock. Once, twice. On the third hit, the wood splintered, and the door swung open, revealing a steep staircase descending into darkness.

A foul smell wafted up—a mix of mildew, sweat, and something metallic. My heart clenched.

I fumbled for the light switch at the top of the stairs and flicked it on. A dim, bare bulb illuminated the scene below.

I descended slowly, my gun drawn, though I knew in my gut no one else was here. The sight that met me at the bottom is one that will haunt me for the rest of my life.

In the cold, damp basement, two figures were chained to opposite walls by their ankles. They were slumped on thin, filthy mattresses. The room was a prison.

It was Ajay and Sital.

But they were shadows of the vibrant young people in the photos. Ajay was painfully thin, his clothes hanging off him, his face gaunt and covered in a scraggly beard. A dirty cloth was tied as a blindfold around his eyes. Sital... Sital's condition was worse. Her face, once so lively, was marred by long, angry red cuts and what looked like burns on one cheek. Her hair was matted. Both were unconscious or sleeping, their breathing shallow.

But they were breathing. They were alive.

A wave of emotion—relief, horror, fury—crashed over me. "Call an ambulance! Now! And get a medical team down here!" I shouted up the stairs.

I moved to Ajay first, gently removing the blindfold. His eyelids fluttered. "It's okay," I whispered, my voice thick. "You're safe. The police are here." I checked the crude chains. They were padlocked. "We need bolt cutters!"

I then went to Sital. She stirred as I approached, whimpering and trying to shrink away. "Sital, it's Inspector Veer Singh. You're safe. We're getting you out." Her eyes, when they opened, were wide with a terror so deep it was soul-shattering.

The next few minutes were a blur of activity. Constables arrived with tools and cut the chains. The paramedics rushed in, carefully assessing the victims, administering oxygen, and starting IV lines. They were loaded onto stretchers and carried up into the blinding daylight, towards the wailing ambulances.

I took one last look at the horrible basement, then followed them out. I had to get back to court.

When I re-entered the courtroom, all conversation ceased. Every eye was on me. The judge leaned forward. "Inspector?"

"We found them, My Lord," I announced, my voice ringing in the silent hall. "Ajay and Sital. They are alive. They have been rescued and are on their way to the hospital."

The reaction was instantaneous. Ajay's mother fainted into her husband's arms. Sital's parents clung to each other, sobbing with relief. Anil put his face in his hands, his shoulders shaking. The room erupted in cheers and applause, which the judge this time did not silence.

When order was restored, the judge turned his steely gaze first to Sonam, who looked broken, then to Vikram Solanki. "So," the judge said, his voice like gravel. "Why did this man confess to a double murder he did not commit?"

Vikram said nothing, staring straight ahead.

"When I saw on the news that someone had been arrested for the kidnapping," Sonam whispered, "I got scared. I still had money from... from my father. I paid this man to confess, to take the blame for everything, so the police would stop looking."

"After hearing all the evidence," the judge pronounced, "under Section 364A of the IPC for kidnapping for ransom and Section 307 for attempted murder, this court sentences Sonam to life imprisonment. Under Section 370 for trafficking, this court sentences Vikram Solanki and Bablu to twenty years of rigorous imprisonment each. The court is adjourned."

The gavel fell with a final, definitive crack.

As the officers led Sonam and Vikram away, the families surrounded me. Ajay's father gripped my hand, tears streaming down his face. "Inspector, how can we ever thank you?"

"You don't need to thank me," I said, feeling emotionally drained. "If you want to thank someone, thank Sital's little sister. Her courage gave us the first real clue."

They nodded, overcame, and were led away by family support officers.

I felt a hand on my arm. It was Ruhi. She looked exhausted but victorious. "Well," she said, a small smile touching her lips. "I think we should get married fast."

I managed a weary laugh. "Why wait? The judge is still here. Let's do it now."

She swatted my arm, and we shared a moment of genuine, relieved laughter amidst the chaos.

I have to tell Dev, I thought.

I drove to the hospital. Dev was sitting in a chair by the window, looking much stronger.

"Oh, recovering fast, I see," I said.

"Sir! Congratulations! We solved it. What an unexpected twist," he said, his smile fading as he saw my expression. "But you don't look happy."

"We solved this case, Dev," I said, sitting down. "But in court, Sonam said nothing about MASTER JI. She cut out a huge part of the story. Her confession was too neat, too focused on personal revenge."

"What? Then how do we find MASTER JI?" Dev asked, his face falling.

"The case is officially closed, but that whole trafficking system is still operating. We have to break it. I need to talk to Sonam again."

"Sir, can I ask you something?" Dev said looking in my eye

"Yes, why not" I said smiling

"What about your previous case, what happened to 3 year little girl"

"It's a whole story dev, I'll tell you some other day, it was a whole novel" I said and laugh

I spent the next hour with Dev, going over the details, our minds already turning to the larger, shadowy enemy. Finally, I took my leave. "Just focus on getting better. That's an order."

My mother called as I was leaving. "Congratulations, my son! You solved the impossible case!"

"Thanks, Mom," I said, the weight of the unsolved questions making the victory feel hollow.

That night, in my own bed, I slept a deep, dreamless sleep for the first time in weeks.

The next day, I visited Ajay and Sital in the hospital. They were in separate, guarded rooms. They were awake, but the trauma in their eyes was profound. Ajay could barely speak, his throat raw from disuse and dehydration. Sital would flinch at sudden movements. The doctors said physical recovery would take weeks; the psychological scars would last much longer.

"It will take time, beta," I said softly to each of them. "But you're safe now."

After speaking with their devastated but grateful parents, I left the hospital. My next stop was the women's prison.

It took thirty minutes to get through the formalities. Finally, I was seated in a visitor's room, separated from the inmates by thick glass. Sonam was brought in. She looked smaller in the prison uniform, her defiance replaced by a weary resignation. She picked up the phone on her side.

"Why?" I asked simply.

"I already told you everything in court," she said flatly.

"I mean, why did you cut out the part about the MASTER JI?"

A slow, knowing smile spread across her face. It was a smile that chilled me to the bone. "Oh. So you know the real story... No one else does. No one knows who MASTER JI really is." She leaned closer to the glass, her voice dropping to a whisper I could barely hear through the receiver. "You know nothing about MASTER JI."

"Everyone says that. He helped you. Bablu's story is real. I know that, Why protect him?"

"Okay," she said, her smile widening into something grotesque. "I'll tell you. It doesn't matter now. No one will believe you anyway." She gestured for me to lean in. I pressed my ear to the glass partition.

"Yes bablu story is real.. Assistant call, promotion to group C everything and I am the one who is there in the car, giving money and ticket to bablu' she said 'and one more thing.... '

Her next words, hissed through the phone, were like a physical blow.

"MASTER JI is my FATHER."

I jerked back. "WHAT?!"

She threw her head back and laughed, a harsh, barking sound that held no joy. "Yes! And I did everything to save my father. I sensed you were getting close, so I confessed to everything—the kidnapping, the imprisonment. I made it a simple crime of passion. A closed case. No more investigations. And what, you think I'll be here for life?" She leaned forward again, her eyes glittering with manic intensity. "MASTER JI always wins. My father's lawyers are the best. Appeals, mental health evaluations... I'll be out in ten years, maybe less. And something big is coming, Inspector. You have no idea."

"Time's up," a guard said behind her.

She gave me one last, terrifying smile, mouthed the word "Father," and was led away, her laughter echoing down the concrete corridor.

I left the prison in a daze. Her father. The pieces shifted again, forming an even more horrifying picture. A father solved his own daughter's jealousy to orchestrate a kidnapping..who was he?

That night, I was trying to process it all when my phone rang. It was a video call. I answered to find a screen split between my family, Dev looking cheerful from his hospital bed, and Ruhi with her parents.

"Sir, what's the time?" Dev asked, grinning.

I checked. "It's 11:55 PM. Why?"

"Sir, it's December 31st. In five minutes, it's the New Year!"

I had completely lost track of the date. A flicker of genuine excitement cut through my gloom. We waited for 4 min and 55 sec then We counted down together across the screens. "Five... four... three... two... one... HAPPY NEW YEAR!"

Cheers and laughter filled the call. "Happy New Year, everyone!" I shouted, a real smile on my face for the first time in what felt like forever.

We chatted for a few more minutes before disconnecting. A new year. New cases, I thought, the smile lingering. And an old, monstrous one still to finish.

Then, my phone rang again. An unknown number. Who could it be now?

I answered. "Hello?"

A dark, digitally altered voice greeted me, devoid of any human warmth. "Happy New Year, Inspector..."

"Happy New Year," I replied cautiously. "I'm sorry, I don't recognize your voice."

"Oh? You don't remember me? Let me give you another guess... No?" The voice paused, letting the silence stretch. "Alright, I'll tell you. Everyone calls me... MASTER JI."

The name was like ice water in my veins. "MASTER JI?" I whispered.

"You are the man because of whom my fourth daughter is in a lockup. You lost me a very important client. It is not a happy new year for me. But for you... I will make sure your whole year is ruined, just like you ruined mine. You think MASTER JI is just a pond you can fish in? It is a whole ocean, Inspector. An ocean that is about to swallow you whole."

He began to laugh, a low, synthesized sound that was more terrifying than any human expression of mirth. Before I could respond, the call disconnected.

My phone buzzed immediately with a notification from my bank app. I opened it, my hands trembling.

Transaction Alert: ₹10,000 CREDITED to your account.

Ten thousand rupees. The exact amount I had given to Raghu, the taxi driver in Dehradun who helped us to catch bablu.

After 5 minutes of thinking I finally realized

I didn't feel fear at that moment. I felt a cold, clarifying rage. I started to laugh, a hard, determined sound. He's paying me. He's telling me he was there. He's telling me the game is still on.

I have to find this "MASTER JI". Sonam's final words echoed in my mind. Something big is coming.

And I would be waiting.

Upcomming Chapter

"he killed all his friends when he was 16," the old man said, looking down sadly.

"What?" I said, confused

"Yes, it's been good if you leave, sir. I don't want to talk about that."

"But why?... You said he read all things about God, including the Bhagavad Gita."

"Yes, but he loves his sister more than anyone," he said, closing his fist hard.

"sister?"

"If I tell you what happened that night. He will become a different person for you."

"I don't think so after what he's done to my family," I said angrily.

"You will never win this fight, I already told you. Forgot that happened to your family and move on," he said

"forgot! after all this.... NO, this is not a fight anymore, this is war! he is the villain of my story."

"VILLEN," he said and laughed, "villain is always be the villain if hero telling the story, sir, you saw this story from your side, now let me tell his story," he said, looking at my eye.

"What do you tell?"

"I will tell you, but you have to promise you don't cry," he said, looking serious

Last Massage

Thank you for reading FHIR KYA HUA?

If you have reached this page, it means you stayed with the story till the end- through every question, every silence, and evey twist. As a first-time writer, that itself means a lot to me.

This story is not just about the case; it is about curiosity, choices, and the truth hidden between them, I hope it kept you engaged and made you think beyond the pages.

But this is not the end.

This is only the begining of my journey as a writer, and there are many more stories waiting to be told.

As they say in cinima-

"Abhi picture baaki hai, mere dost"

Thank you for being a part of this case.

-Gaurav Singh Negi

www.ingramcontent.com/pod-product-compliance
Lightning Source LLC
LaVergne TN
LVHW100306210926
848480LV00003B/1037